Anne & Gilbert

Book and Lyrics by
Jeff Hochhauser

Music and Lyrics by
Bob Johnston and Nancy White

A SAMUEL FRENCH ACTING EDITION

SAMUEL
FRENCH
FOUNDED 1830
NEW YORK HOLLYWOOD LONDON TORONTO
SAMUELFRENCH.COM

IMPORTANT BILLING AND CREDIT REQUIREMENTS

All producers of *ANNE & GILBERT* *must* give credit to the Author of the Play in all programs distributed in connection with performances of the Play, and in all instances in which the title of the Play appears for the purposes of advertising, publicizing or otherwise exploiting the Play and/or a production. The name of the Author *must* appear on a separate line on which no other name appears, immediately following the title and *must* appear in size of type not less than fifty percent of the size of the title type.

ANNE & GILBERT: A MUSICAL had its world premiere on August 4, 2005 at the Victoria Playhouse in Victoria-By-the-Sea, Prince Edward Island, Canada. It was produced for Campbell Webster Entertainment by Campbell Webster and David Malahoff. The director and choreographer was Duncan McIntosh, with musical direction by Lisa St. Clair, orchestrations by Tom Leighton and Bob Johnston, set design by John Craig Dinning, costume design by Phillip Clarkson, and lighting design by Elizabeth Asselstine. The band was Lisa St. Clair, Mark Haines and Julia McLaine, and the cast was as follows:

JOSIE PYE . . . . Natalie Sullivan

GILBERT BLYTHE . . . . Peter Deiwick

MR. SLOANE/STATIONMASTER/REVEREND/PROFESSOR/HEAD WAITER . . . . Erskine Smith

RACHEL LYNDE . . . . Pam Stevenson

ANNE SHIRLEY . . . . Marla McLean

DIANA BARRY/REDMOND STUDENT . . . . Sarah Sheps

FRED WRIGHT/REDMOND STUDENT . . . . Christopher Gillis

MARILLA CUTHBERT . . . . Laura Smith

MOODY SPURGEON MACPHERSON . . . . John Connolly

PAUL IRVING . . . . Brandon Banks

PRILLIE ROGERSON/REDMOND STUDENT . . . . Brittany Banks

BARBARA SHAW/REDMOND STUDENT . . . . Isabel MacDougall

ANNETTA BELL/REDMOND STUDENT . . . . Whitney Rose

ALEC/ANTHONY PYE . . . . Jesse Martyn

ALONZO/AVONLEA PUPIL . . . . Nick Whelan

PHILIPPA GORDON/AVONLEA PUPIL . . . . Maria Campbell

ROY GARDNER/BENJI SLOANE . . . . Sean C. Robertson

CHARACTERS

ANNE SHIRLEY – 19. Anne of Green Gables at 19. A beautiful and fiery redhead, charming, impulsive, charismatic and very intelligent. Wise beyond her years about everything and everybody except Gilbert.

GILBERT BLYTHE – 20. The best looking and smartest guy in town. He is deeply in love with Anne and determined to win her.

MARILLA CUTHBERT – 50s. Anne's guardian. She used to be a lot crustier but her years with Anne have brought out her warmth and humour.

MRS. LYNDE – 50s. The town busybody. A loveable know it all.

JOSIE PYE – 20. As close to a bad girl as you can get in Avonlea. Sexy, funny and good-hearted underneath her bluster.

PHILIPPA GORDON – 20. A beautiful and sophisticated if somewhat giddy heiress.

MOODY SPURGEON MACPHERSON – 20, goofy suitor fo Anne's who wants to be a minister. The actor in this role must play the fiddle/violin.

ROY GARDNER – 22. A handsome and very wealthy college boy. Used to getting what he wants. And he wants Anne.

DIANA BARRY – 19. Anne's best friend. Spunky, adorable and very down-to-earth.

PAUL IRVING – 10. Anne's favourite pupil. Polite and very smart but desperate to fit in.

ANTHONY PYE – 12. Anne's least favourite pupil. Usually in trouble.

MR. SLOANE – 50s. Also plays a starchy head waiter and the minister.

ALEC & ALONZO – Two rich college boys, madly in love with Philippa. One of them will also play **DIANA**'s fiancee **FRED WRIGHT**.

NOTES ON CASTING

ANNE & GILBERT can be performed by a cast of 17 or more.

In a production where a children's chorus is added, the adult cast can be reduced to 14.

SETTING

ACT ONE is set in Avonlea, a small village on Prince Edward Island in the Canadian Maritimes. It is 1881.

ACT TWO is set mostly at Redmond University in Halifax. It is 1882.

SYNOPSIS OF SCENES AND MUSICAL NUMBERS

Act I

The entire first act takes place in the village of Avonlea, on Prince Edward Island in the Canadian Maritimes. 1881.

Scene 1: Outside the schoolhouse

"Mr. Blythe" . . . . Josie and the girls of Avonlea

"Gilbert Loves Anne of Green Gables" . . . . Mrs. Lynde, Mr. Sloane, Mrs. Pye

"Averil's Ideal" . . . . Anne

"Carried Away By Love" . . . . . Gilbert, Anne, Moody and ensemble

Scene 2: The Green Gables kitchen

Scene 3: Inside the schoolhouse

Scene 4: Outside the schoolhouse

"You're Island Through and Through" Gilbert, Anne and ensemble

"Polishing Silver" . . . . Anne and Diana

Scene 5: A small beach cove

"Saturday Morning" . . . . Gilbert

"Hello, Gilbert!" . . . . Josie and Gilbert

Scene 6: The graveyard

"All You Can Do Is Wait" . . . . Gilbert

Scene 7: Green Gables, then the schoolhouse

"A Jonah Day" . . . . Anne, Josie, Paul, Anthony and students

Scene 8: The Carmody train station

"Our Duty" . . . . Marilla and Mrs. Lynde

Scene 9: Outside the schoolhouse

"Averil's Ideal" (reprise) . . . . Diana

"Someone Handed Me the Moon" . . . . Anne

Scene 10: Diana's wedding

"Blessed Be the Avonlea Bride" . . . . Ensemble

"Carried Away By Love" (reprise) . . . . Anne and Gilbert

Act II

The entire second act takes place at Redmond University except where indicated. 1882.

Scene 1: The campus

"The Days Ahead" . . . . Anne, Gilbert, Phil, Roy and Ensemble

Scene 2: Old St. John's Cemetery

"Seesaw Girl" . . . . .Phil, Alec and Alonzo

"When He Was My Beau" . . . . Marilla

Scene 3: Underneath a tree, outside the cemetery

"May I Offer My Umbrella?" . . . . Roy and Anne

Scene 4: Avonlea

"Gilbert Would Never Compose a Sonnet To My Eyes" . . Diana and Anne

"You're Never Safe From Surprises Till You're Dead" . . Mrs. Lynde

"Hello, Gilbert!" (reprise) . . . . .Josie

Scene 5: A ladies' dressing room

"Hothouse Flower" . . . . Gilbert and co-eds

Scene 6: A formal reception

"Just When I'd Given Up Hope" . .Roy, Josie, Gilbert and ensemble

"You're Island Through and Through" (reprise). . . . Gilbert, Josie, Anne, Moody and ensemble

Scene 7: Outside the reception

"That Little Fiddle Player" . . . . .Phil, Alec, Alonzo and Moody

Scene 8: Charlotte's Café

"Forever In My Life" . . . . Anne

Scene 9: Avonlea

"Finale". . . . . .Ensemble

From the original producers of *Anne & Gilbert*...

ANNE & GILBERT is an unusual Canadian theatre story. Since its launch in 2005 it has become the most successful and critically acclaimed new musical in Canada in recent memory. With rave reviews in *Variety*, *The Toronto Star*, *The Ottawa Citizen* and countless other publications, it has accomplished in tiny Prince Edward Island, Canada's smallest province, what few other Canadian musicals have achieved anywhere.

Its popularity in Canadian theatres is owing to a small army of enthusiasts, none more important than the three gifted writers who started it all: Jeff Hochhauser, Bob Johnston and Nancy White. Their adaptation for the stage of L.M. Montgomery's classic novels has been brought to life by many excellent performers, directors and designers.

None of *Anne & Gilbert's* success would have happened without the original investors in the production: Fred Hyndman, Doug Hall, Peter MacDougald and David Carmody. Their early support made *Anne & Gilbert* possible.

Campbell Webster
David Malahoff

Producers/ANNE & GILBERT

ACKNOWLEDGEMENTS

A musical with a cast of seventeen is a big animal, and before it even gets produced, its writers become indebted to the hundreds of people who help with its development. *Anne & Gilbert* was workshopped in New York, Toronto and Charlottetown at least eight times, and performers took part for the love of theatre. We thank them, and of course the actors, musicians, crew people, administrators and investors who got the show on the road. We especially extend affectionate thanks to our producers, Campbell Webster and David Malahoff who made our dream their nightmare! And we'd also like to extend un gros merci to the following folks and institutions who helped with the writers' creative process.

Albert Ahronheim, The American Musical and Dramatic Academy, Pat Anweiler, Jill Corey, Michael Fletcher, Heidi Ford, Tim French, Maurice & Mary Gallant, Jessica Grové, Howard K.Hamm, Jr., Mark Haines, Carol Hanzel, The Harbourfront Jubilee Theatre, Sean Kemp (for violin advice), Dale Koshida, Jeffrey Landsman, Tom Leighton, John McKellar, Ann Merriam, James Morgan, David Myers (for appreciated musical input), Richard Ouzounian, Erskine & Pat Smith, The Victoria Playhouse, Greg Wanless, Wexford Collegiate School for the Arts, The York Theatre Company, and, of course, the brilliant Lucy Maud Montgomery.

— *Jeff Hochhauser, Bob Johnston and Nancy White*

ACT 1

Scene One

(Outside the school. Late summer.)

*(***JOSIE PYE*** and a bunch of young ***GIRLS*** of various ages look longingly at the school.)*

GIRLS.

EVERY YOUNG GIRL IN AVONLEA
IS ABOUT AS CLOSE TO HEAVEN
AS SHE CAN BE
IF YOU DON'T KNOW WHY
THEN I GUESS YOU DIDN'T HEAR
MR. BLYTHE
WHO MAKES THE GIRLS OF AVONLEA SIGH
MR. BLYTHE
THE BEST LOOKING BOY ON P.E.I.
MR. BLYTHE

JOSIE.

IS GONNA BE MY TEACHER
THIS YEAR

GIRLS.

ONCE IN A WHILE I'LL BREAK A RULE
SO TEACHER WILL BE FORCED
TO KEEP ME AFTER SCHOOL
PLEASE VACATION END
FOR THE FUN BEGINS IN FALL

MR. BLYTHE
SITTIN' ON HIS DESK RECITIN' RHYMES
MR. BLYTHE
NO ONE CUTER IN THE MARITIMES
MR. BLYTHE
I NEVER WANT TO GRADUATE
AT ALL

(GILBERT comes up the path headed for the school. The GIRLS' eyes light up as he passes.)

FIRST GIRL. Good afternoon, Mr. Blythe.

SECOND GIRL. Good afternoon, Mr. Blythe.

THIRD GIRL. Good afternoon, Mr. Blythe.

JOSIE. *(provocatively)* Hello, Gilbert!

GILBERT. *(with a devastating smile)* Goodbye, Josie.

(GILBERT goes into the school. The GIRLS fairly swoon.)

JOSIE. *(as the rest of the GIRLS sing answer back-up)*

MR. BLYTHE
MR. BLYTHE
YOU'RE NOT JUST BEAUTIFUL

MR. BLYTHE
MR. BLYTHE
YOU'RE NOT JUST WONDERFUL TO SEE

MR. BLYTHE
MR. BLYTHE
IN MY HEART OF HEARTS

JOSIE & GIRLS.

YOU WILL ALWAYS BE GILBERT TO ME
EVERY DAY WE'LL DRESS UP AND YOU CAN BET
WE'LL BE TRYING
WE'LL BE VYING
TO BE THE TEACHER'S PET
EVEN WITH THE FLU
WE'LL GO TO SCHOOL EVERY DAY
MR. BLYTHE
NOW YOU'RE MY TEACHER
YOU'RE A MAN
MR. BLYTHE
I'LL DO MY HOMEWORK
WHEN I CAN
MR. BLYTHE
IF ONLY YOU'D GET OVER

(as if it were a dirty word)

ANNE!

JOSIE. (GIRLS *again sing answer back up.*)

> MR. BLYTHE
> MR. BLYTHE
> YOU'RE NOT JUST BEAUTIFUL
> MR. BLYTHE
> MR. BLYTHE
> YOU'RE NOT JUST WONDERFUL TO SEE
>
> MR. BLYTHE
> MR. BLYTHE

GIRLS.

> MR. TEACHER

JOSIE.

> YOU WILL ALWAYS BE GILBERT

JOSIE & GIRLS.

> I LOVE YOU GILBERT
> YOU WILL ALWAYS BE GILBERT
> TO ME

> *(Lights come up inside the schoolhouse.)*

> **(GILBERT** *is addressing the Avonlea School Board which consists of* **MRS. LYNDE, MR. SLOANE** *and* **MRS. PYE.***)*

GILBERT. I cannot begin to express my gratitude that the Avonlea School Board has accepted my application to become your new schoolmaster.
> I love this school.
> Seems like only yesterday I was a student here.

MRS. LYNDE. It was!

GILBERT. That is almost true, Mrs. Lynde!
> So it's very difficult to have to tell you this: The White Sands School has offered me substantially more money and if I'm to save the tuition to attend university next year....I cannot afford the pleasure of teaching in Avonlea this year.

MRS. LYNDE. Well! You're never safe from surprises till you're dead!

MRS. PYE. Doesn't speak so well of Avonlea that our schoolmasters teach BEFORE they go to university.

MRS. LYNDE. *(proudly)* Hush, Mrs. Pye! It's the Canadian way!

MR. SLOANE. Not like you, Gilbert, leavin' Avonlea in the lurch only a week before school starts!

GILBERT. Mr. Sloane, sir, I would never have accepted the position at White Sands were it not for the fact that ANNE SHIRLEY is available.

MRS. PYE. That red-headed orphan from the Cuthbert farm?

MRS. LYNDE. That 'red-headed orphan' gave up a full scholarship at Redmond University to stay home and care for Marilla Cuthbert!

I say let's put the hiring of Anne Shirley to a vote! AGREED?

MRS. PYE. AYE!

MRS. LYNDE. AYE!

MR. SLOANE. I'M chairman of this committee! I decide when we vote.

MRS. LYNDE. Jake Sloane, you're being.....Sloanish!

MR. SLOANE. Gilbert! You're fired!

GILBERT. Excellent!

MR. SLOANE. Is that un-Sloanish enough for you, Rachel Lynde?

GILBERT. *(rushing off)* Thank you.

MRS. PYE. *(once* **GILBERT** *is gone)* I find it embarrassing that the White Sands school pays its teachers 'substantially' more than Avonlea!

MRS. LYNDE. They more than likely pay less!

MRS. PYE. White Sands pays LESS? I'm lost.

MRS. LYNDE.

THE GRASS POPS UP IN THE PASTURE
THE BREAKERS BREAK ON THE SHORE
YOU GET YOUR EGGS FROM A CHICKEN
YOU GET YOUR NEWS AT THE STORE
SOME THINGS YOU KNOW FOR CERTAIN
NO ONE QUESTIONS ANYMORE

GILBERT LOVES ANNE OF GREEN GABLES
AND THOUGH SHE WON'T ADMIT IT'S TRUE
ANNE OF GREEN GABLES LOVES GILBERT TOO

MRS. PYE.

HE MET THAT GIRL IN THE CLASSROOM
HE LOVED THAT GIRL FROM THE START

MR. SLOANE.

THEY SEEMED TO BE BORN TO BATTLE
LIKE THE SLOANES

MRS. PYE.

AND THE PYES

MRS. LYNDE.

ONLY SMART

ALL THREE.

SOMEBODY NEEDS TO TELL THEM

MRS. LYNDE.

THEY SHOULD NEVER BE APART

*(***MRS. LYNDE, MRS. PYE*** and* **MR. SLOANE** *go.)*

(Outside the school house where **DIANA, FRED** *and* **TOWNSPEOPLE** *are walking by.)*

ALL.

GILBERT LOVES ANNE OF GREEN GABLES
AND THOUGH SHE MAKES A BIG TO-DO
ANNE OF GREEN GABLES LOVES GILBERT TOO

MRS. LYNDE.

HE WORSHIPS THE GROUND SHE WALKS ON
AS ANYONE CAN SEE
SHE TREATS HIM LIKE HER DEAR OLD DOG
SHE'S FOOLING HERSELF
BUT SHE'S NOT FOOLING ME

MRS. PYE.

THE GIRLS IN TOWN ADORE HIM
THEY WON'T LEAVE GILBERT ALONE

MR. SLOANE.

BUT GILBERT WILL CONQUER HIS SWEETHEART

MRS. LYNDE.

AS SURE AS A PYE'LL CHEAT A SLOANE

ALL.

SOME THINGS ARE WRIT IN GRANITE

MRS LYNDE.

SOMEWHERE THIS IS CARVED IN STONE:

ALL.

(as the **GIRLS** *sing* MR. BLYTHE*)*

GILBERT LOVES ANNE OF GREEN GABLES

AND ALL OF US HAVE ALWAYS KNOWN

ANNE OF GREEN GABLES IS GILBERT'S OWN

GILBERT LOVES ANNE OF GREEN GABLES

AND THOUGH SHE'LL BE THE LAST TO KNOW

ANNE OF GREEN GABLES LOVES GILBERT SO

GILBERT LOVES ANNE OF GREEN GABLES

GILBERT LOVES ANNE OF GREEN GABLES

AND ANNE OF GREEN GABLES LOVES GILBERT SO

(Toward the end of the above chorus, a beautiful nineteen year-old redhead comes up the path reading a letter.)

(On the last note of the song, she is revealed to be **ANNE SHIRLEY.** *And she is NOT pleased about what her neighbours are singing.)*

*(***ANNE***'s best friend* **DIANA** *rushes to meet her.)*

ANNE. WHY do they do it, Diana? WHY does half of Avonlea insist that Gilbert and I are in love?

DIANA. Oh Anne, it's more than half!

ANNE. *(stewing for a moment as she digests this, then)* Well I'm sorry to disappoint you and more than half of Avonlea!

Gilbert is a good chum. That's all!

DIANA. Then why are you blushing?

ANNE. I am not!

DIANA. You always blush whenever anybody mentions Gilbert.

ANNE. It doesn't mean I'm in love. It means I'm embarrassed!

DIANA. If you say so.

ANNE. I could never love Gilbert Blythe!

I'm too much like Averil.

DIANA. From your short story?

ANNE. From my failed short story!

DIANA. How can you call it failed? It's beautiful!

ANNE. I just picked this up at the post office.

Rejected!

And by *CANADIAN WOMAN!*

When you've been rejected by *CANADIAN WOMAN....* there's no hope!

DIANA. I've been thinking you might enter it in the Rollings Reliable Baking Powder Literary Competition.

ANNE. *(a little grandly)* There isn't a WORD in my story about BAKING POWDER!

DIANA. But there could be!

You could just slip it in somewhere!

(defensively)

It really is an excellent product.

ANNE. To me that story is sacred!

(Music begins.)

DIANA. It's my favourite of everything you've written.

ANNE. *(opening her manuscript)* Mine too.

'WHEN AVERIL WAS A SWEET YOUNG THING
HER FRIENDS WERE ALWAYS WHISPERING
OF BEAUX THEY'D HAD AND BEAUX TO COME
BUT AVERIL KEPT HER PEACE
FOR SHE KNEW THERE WAS MORE TO LIFE
THAN SETTLING DOWN AS SOMEONE'S WIFE
SHE MIGHT BE LONELY, THIS SHE KNEW
BUT SHE HAD THINGS TO DO
THIS WAS HER CAPRICE
AVERIL KEPT HER PEACE

WHEN AVERIL WAS BUT SEVENTEEN
A HANDSOME LAD CAME ON THE SCENE
AND HE WAS SMART AND FAIR AND KIND

BUT AVERIL TURNED AWAY
THE SIGNS WERE WRONG, SHE WANTED MORE
WHY HE WAS JUST THE BOY NEXT DOOR
AND SHE COULD ONLY FIND ROMANCE
IN PERFECT CIRCUMSTANCE
JUST LIKE IN A PLAY
AVERIL TURNED AWAY

THERE HAD TO BE A TREE
THERE HAD TO BE SOME RAIN
A STRANGER WOULD APPEAR
EXOTIC AND URBANE
AND AVERIL WOULD KNOW
AND AVERIL WOULD FEEL
THIS GENTLEMAN WAS TRULY
AVERIL'S IDEAL'

(ANNE & DIANA sigh.)

It truly IS my most romantic story!

DIANA. All except the part about Averil being an old maid
for sixty years till she finally meets the Dream Man.

That might be all right for you, you're always going to
be divinely slim.

I'm going to be fat!

ANNE. DIANA!

DIANA. Well, I am. My mother is fat! Every single one of my
aunts is fat!

There's nothing romantic about a fat old maid!

ANNE. *(handing DIANA the manuscript)* I want you to keep it.

DIANA. I'll treasure it always.

But Anne, would you REALLY wait sixty years for some
'ideal man'?

Gilbert seems like an awfully good compromise to me!

ANNE.

I THINK I'D NEED A TREE
AND YES, I'D WANT SOME RAIN
AND HE'D BE STANDING THERE

EXOTIC AND URBANE
AND IN A FLASH I'D KNOW
AND IN A FLASH I'D FEEL
I GUESS I'D BE LIKE AVERIL
FINDING MY IDEAL

AND IN A FLASH I'D KNOW
AND IN A FLASH I'D FEEL
I GUESS I'D BE LIKE AVERIL
FINDING MY IDEAL

DIANA. But Gilbert just gave up the Avonlea schoolmaster job.

For you!

ANNE. ME?

DIANA. YOU'RE going to teach at Avonlea, HE's going to teach all the way out at White Sands, so you can stay here and look after Green Gables and Marilla!

It sounded terribly romantic to me.

(romantically)

The handsome young hero gives up

(pragmatically)

an extremely convenient job,

(romantically again)

for the sake of the woman he loves!

Gilbert would do anything for you, Anne. You have to know that!

(GILBERT rushes on.)

GILBERT. ALL RIGHT, ANNE....LET ME HAVE IT!

I went behind your back! I didn't consult you first!

BUT IF I HAD ASKED YOU before I did it....what would you have said?

ANNE & DIANA. 'Don't you dare under any circumstance!'

(ANNE gives DIANA a dirty look.)

DIANA. I'm going to excuse myself now.

ANNE. Diana....

DIANA. Good luck, Gil! Bye Anne.

(**DIANA** *rushes off. There is an uncomfortable moment.*)

GILBERT. Now, Anne, I can come home from White Sands every night because I have a horse.

You, rather appropriately, only have a mule!

(*A moment.* **ANNE** *seems to be weighing her options.*)

ANNE. (*finally and firmly*) Thank you, Gilbert!

GILBERT. That's it? You're not going to yell at me?

ANNE. No, I am not.

It really was a very generous thing to do.

GILBERT. It was rather, wasn't it?

And yet, somehow I get the feeling you're not altogether pleased!

Especially because it's me who's come to your rescue.

ANNE. (*trying really hard to stay calm*) Rescue?

GILBERT. In a manner of speaking.

ANNE. If I'm 'not pleased,' it is not because of YOU.

It's….a story rejection.

GILBERT. "Averil's Ideal?"

ANNE. How do you know about that?

GILBERT. Diana let Fred read it and he lent it to me.

ANNE. Diana wasn't supposed to show that to anyone! Did you like it?

GILBERT. (*uncomfortably*) Ummm,

I've always thought you were a very talented writer.

I think you ought to write about yourself.

ANNE. Who would want to read a book about Anne of Green Gables?

You didn't like it!

GILBERT. Well…no.

It just isn't realistic!

Imagine you, Anne, waiting sixty years for some Mr. Ideal!

ANNE. I can easily imagine that. Considering my options!

GILBERT. You're way too smart to live in some fake romantic dream world!

Come on, Anne, whatever reverie you go off in,

you know in your heart when the chips are down,

it's me you're going to marry!

(pause)

ANNE. You egotistical –

GILBERT. You wouldn't care to make a small friendly wager?

ANNE. A wager, Gilbert?

GILBERT. *(taking a gold coin out of his pocket)* I'll bet my lucky gold piece.

My dad gave it to me when I was sixteen.

Just as his dad gave it to him.

ANNE. And the terms of this friendly wager?

GILBERT. I will propose marriage to you at some future moment of my choosing –

ANNE. It won't be mine!

GILBERT. If you say 'no!' you have my word of honour, I will NEVER ask you again!

And, my lucky gold piece.

ANNE. And what could I possibly wager against the easiest gold piece I'm ever going to win?

*(Big smile from **ANNE**.)*

GILBERT. Just your heart, Anne! That's all I've ever wanted.

*(Neither of them notices **MARILLA** coming down the path.)*

ANNE. *(The smile is gone.)* Oh, you THINK you know exactly what a girl wants to hear, don't you?

GILBERT. It's a bewildering gift!

ANNE. YOU DON'T HAVE THE SLIGHTEST IDEA, GILBERT BLYTHE!

So I will take that wager!

I will take that wager because there is more chance of my getting engaged to THAT TREE!

MARILLA. ANNE SHIRLEY!

ANNE. *(mortified)* Hello, Marilla.

MARILLA. Is this the way I brought you up to behave?

ANNE. *(She thinks this over, then)* Not exactly.

MARILLA. And after what Gilbert's just done for you.
And for me.

Thank you very kindly, Gilbert.

GILBERT. Anytime I can be of service, Miss Cuthbert.

(Under her breath, **ANNE** *imitates him.)*

MARILLA. ANNE SHIRLEY!

Gilbert gave up the Avonlea schoolmaster job for you.
It seems to me that you could at least ACT beholden
to him,

(heading home)

for ONE evening!

(pause)

GILBERT. *(asking* **MARILLA***)* For one WHOLE evening?

(After a moment, **MARILLA** *nods and rushes off.)*

ANNE. If Marilla says I have to, I suppose I have to!

(A group of young people have gathered around **MOODY
SPURGEON,** *a rather dour looking young man who
starts to play his fiddle. One couple after another begin
to dance.)*

GILBERT. *(suddenly serious)* Since you're in such an obliging
state of mind – I plan to keep up my studies, even if I
can't go to university yet.
I assume you do too.

ANNE. For once you assume correctly.

GILBERT. Then let's be study partners. I for one could use
the help.
What do you say, Anne?

ANNE. That's an offer that makes too much common sense
to refuse.

GILBERT. Oh, I don't mean to be TOO common sensical!
How about a dance?

ANNE. I don't care what Marilla says! I'm not THAT grateful!

GILBERT. Oh, come on, Anne, Moody's started in on his fiddle.

He won't be around to play for us much longer.

ANNE. I know. This time next week he'll be at university.

GILBERT. We'll get there too, Anne. You'll see! Now how about that dance?

ANNE. I really don't care to.

GILBERT.

LOOK AT THE LOVERS
AREN'T THEY A PICTURE?
DANCING SO FINE
UNDER THE MOONLIGHT
ALMOST AS IN A TRANCE
UNDER THE SPELL OF THE DANCE
CARRIED AWAY BY LOVE

THEY HEAR THE MUSIC
THEY FEEL THE MOONLIGHT
THEY DON'T RESIST
LISTEN IT'S CALLING
DARE YOU TO DANCE WITH ME
WE'RE NOT THE KIND WHO COULD BE
CARRIED AWAY BY LOVE

CARRIED AWAY BY STARS IN THE SKY
CARRIED AWAY BY DREAMS
CARRIED AWAY BY LOVE, YOU AND I?
WE'RE NOT THE KIND INCLINED TO GET CARRIED AWAY

GILBERT. *(cont.)*

THERE WILL BE TALK IF UNDER THE MOONLIGHT
WE ARE THE ONES TALKING NOT DANCING
PRIVACY'S NOT ALLOWED
SMARTER TO FOLLOW THE CROWD
CARRIED AWAY BY LOVE

*(**ANNE** and **GILBERT** finally join the dance.)*

ALL EXCEPT ANNE & GILBERT.

LOOK AT THE LOVERS
AREN'T THEY A PICTURE?
DANCING SO FINE
UNDER THE MOONLIGHT
ALMOST AS IN A TRANCE
UNDER THE SPELL OF THE DANCE
CARRIED AWAY BY LOVE

ALL EXCEPT ANNE.

UNDER THE SPELL OF THE DANCE

(During the above, **ANNE** *breaks away from* **GILBERT** *and goes off.)*

GILBERT.

CARRIED AWAY BY LOVE

*(***GILBERT** *and the rest of the* **YOUNG PEOPLE** *go off in different directions as* **MOODY** *finishes his fiddling.)*

(Lights come up on the Green Gables kitchen.)

Scene Two

(Green Gables kitchen.)

ANNE. Oh, Marilla, my pupils are just waiting for me to fail!

MARILLA. You will hardly fail completely in one day and there's plenty more days coming.

There's the trouble with you, Anne, is you'll expect to teach those children everything and reform all their faults right off.

ANNE. It wouldn't be so terrible if I were to be teaching children who didn't know me.

Most of my pupils were my old school mates.

How am I to get them to respect me the way they would a stranger?

How am I to get them to call me 'Miss Shirley?'

MRS. LYNDE. *(barging in and offering an opinion)* You've got to whoop one!

ANNE. MRS. LYNDE!

MRS. LYNDE. As an example!

The first one that acts up, you show your class a whooping they won't forget!

ANNE. I could never whoop, WHIP a child!

MRS. LYNDE. Our teachers always whooped a student, first day of school. Isn't that so, Marilla?

MARILLA. Usually one of the Pyes.

MRS. LYNDE. Now I come to think of it, one year it was YOU, Marilla!

MARILLA. RACHEL LYNDE!

ANNE. *(stunned)* Why, Marilla, what could you have done?

MRS. LYNDE. She was passing love notes with her beau, John Blythe!

(MARILLA shoots MRS. LYNDE the dirtiest look ever!)

ANNE. You and Gilbert's father, Marilla? Really?

MARILLA. *(after a moment)* It was a long time ago.

MRS. LYNDE. *(Realizes she's said something she shouldn't.)* Now, Anne Shirley, never mind about what's none of your business!

You stop in the woods and lay in a supply of switches.

ANNE. I am going to rule by affection, Mrs. Lynde!

MRS. LYNDE. SPARE THE ROD AND SPOIL THE CHILD!

ANNE. Things have changed since your day, Mrs. Lynde. The Earth has cooled!

MRS. LYNDE. You're a very stubborn girl, Anne. We'll see. Some day you'll get riled up.

People with hair like yours are desperate apt to get riled.

MARILLA. You do have a temper.

ANNE. If I can't get along without whipping, I won't teach. I shall try to win my pupils' affection and they will WANT to do what I tell them.

MRS. LYNDE. But suppose they don't?

*(With no answer to that, **ANNE** walks on, shaking her head. **MRS. LYNDE** cackles. **MARILLA** shoots her a look that says BIG MOUTH!)*

(Lights come up on the schoolhouse.)

Scene Three

(Inside the schoolhouse.)

(The **GIRLS**, *led by* **JOSIE** *enter as the* **BOYS** *bring on the school room.)*

JOSIE & GIRLS. *(singing defiantly, under* **JOSIE**'s *instigation)*
EVERY YOUNG GIRL IN AVONLEA
IS AS CLOSE TO SUICIDE AS A GIRL CAN BE
IF YOU DON'T KNOW WHY
THEN I GUESS YOU DIDN'T HEAR

*(***ANNE** *enters the classroom. At least one girl drops out of the chorus and takes her seat.* **ANNE** *crosses her arms. Two more girls drop out of the chorus and sit down.)*

JOSIE & PRILLIE.

MR. BLYTHE
WHO MAKES THE GIRLS OF AVONLEA SIGH
MR. BLYTHE
THE BEST LOOKING BOY ON PEI

*(***ANNE** *points at* **PRILLIE**'s *seat.* **PRILLIE** *loses her nerve, stops singing and sits down.)*

JOSIE.

MR. BLYTHE
AIN'T GONNA BE MY TEACHER
THIS YEAR

(She sits down.)

ANNE. 'Mr. Blythe ISN'T going to be your teacher this year.'
Lucky, Mr. Blythe.

I see a new face in our classroom.

You must be Paul Irving.

PAUL. Yes, ma'am.

ANNE. *(delighted by his manners)* Oh!
My name is...Miss Shirley.

*(***JOSIE** *snickers. This causes others to break up.* **ANNE** *chooses to let this one slide.)*

ANNE. Paul, why don't you introduce yourself to the class?

PAUL. My name is Paul Irving.

I come from the Boston States.

History is my best subject.

And my favourite poet is Yeats.

ANTHONY. 'MY FAVOURITE POET IS YEATS!'

(There is merriment among the PUPILS.)

ANNE. THAT'S ENOUGH!

(to PAUL)

He's one of my favourites too! Paul, you are what I call a kindred spirit! All right, class, let's get to work.

Annetta Bell,

(ANNETTA stands up.)

if you had ten red candies in your right hand, and sixteen green candies in the your left hand, how many candies would you have?

ANNETTA. A mouthful!

(The STUDENTS laugh. ANNE realizes that something is up.)

ANNE. Prillie Rogerson,

(PRILLIE stands.)

What would you like to be when you grow up?

PRILLIE. A widow.

(The STUDENTS howl. Now ANNE knows what's up and takes the bull by the horns.)

ANNE. Josie Pye!

(JOSIE stands.)

Spell 'speckled.'

JOSIE. S...P...I can't spell it, but I can give you an awfully good example of it.

ANNE. All right.

JOSIE. Your face.

(The **STUDENTS** *oooooh!)*

ANNE. Josie, I am the first to appreciate what an adjustment it must be when a former classmate becomes your school teacher! Especially when she's younger than you are. And she knows all of your tricks!

All of them, Josie! Which makes your new teacher fairly confident, that whether you intend to or not,

you are going to have an excellent scholastic year!

And one more thing: another reason you're likely to have a successful school year is because for the first time since you were five,

you won't be able to spend every single moment of the school day throwing yourself at Gilbert Blythe!

Why, who knows, Josie?

This year...you might even finally GRADUATE!

Class, you can close your mouths and open your readers.

(Lights come up on the schoolhouse exterior.)

Scene Four

(Outside the schoolhouse.)

*(**MOODY** is peeking through the keyhole trying to get a glimpse of **ANNE** as **MRS. LYNDE** enters.)*

MRS. LYNDE. Moody Spurgeon MacPherson!
What are you doing here?

*(He's about to say but **MRS. LYNDE** has her own opinion.)*

You've come moonin' over Anne Shirley.
Again!

*(**MOODY**, embarrassed, rushes off. **MRS. LYNDE** is looking through the keyhole herself as **ANNE** comes out the door.)*

MRS. LYNDE. Did you whoop one?

ANNE. No, Mrs. Lynde.

*(The **STUDENTS** start to file out.)*

Goodbye, Barbara.

BARBARA. Goodbye, Miss Shirley.

ANNE. Goodbye, Artie.

ARTIE. Goodbye, Miss Shirley.

*(Sullen little **ANTHONY PYE** comes out the door.)*

ANNE. Goodbye, Anthony.

(He ignores her.)

ANTHONY PYE, I SAID 'GOODBYE!'

ANTHONY. I heard you!

MRS. LYNDE. *(to **ANNE**)* MMMM HMMM!

*(**PRILLIE** & **JOSIE** come out giggling.)*

PRILLIE. You wouldn't dare!

JOSIE. Wouldn't I?

ANNE. Goodbye, Prillie.

PRILLIE. Goodbye, Miss Shirley.

ANNE. Goodbye, Josie.

JOSIE. Goodbye, ANNE!

MRS. LYNDE. Should'a whooped THAT one!

(ANNE decides to let that one go by for now as a triumphant JOSIE rushes off followed by a giggling PRILLIE. During the above, PAUL enters and waits his turn to talk to ANNE. BENJI SLOANE intentionally steps on PAUL's toe. PAUL grimaces silently.)

ANNE. BENJI SLOANE!!!!

(MRS. LYNDE swats him with her handbag and chases him off.)

PAUL. My grandmother keeps telling me: 'Paul, remember you're in Avonlea now!

People aren't quite as outspoken here as in America.'

Grandmother's obviously never met you.

ANNE. I think I'm to take that as a compliment.

PAUL. Oh, yes, ma'am!

ANNE. This must be quite a change from the States!

PAUL. It is different from Boston. But it's where my father grew up.

And my poor little mother is buried here.

(GILBERT lopes into the schoolyard.)

GILBERT. ANNE!

ANNE. You've galloped back to Avonlea rather quickly.

GILBERT. I always will.

ANNE. How was your first day educating the young minds of White Sands?

GILBERT. I don't think it any great exaggeration to say: they loved me!

(a big smile)

And how was your first day educating the young minds of Avonlea?

ANNE. Well...

Meet Paul Irving. He's new to Avonlea from the Boston States.

(**MOODY SPURGEON** *makes a beeline toward* **ANNE.**)

GILBERT. *(to* **PAUL***)* New to Avonlea?

Young fellow, has your teacher taught you much about our island?

PAUL. The subject never came up.

GILBERT. Miss Shirley, the boy needs to know!

ANNE. And I call myself a teacher!

Gilbert, let's enlighten the boy!

GILBERT. Moody!

(**MOODY** *begins a fiddle tune. As the song progresses, many of* **ANNE***'s* **PUPILS, MRS. LYNDE** *and other* **TOWNSPEOPLE** *join them, attracted by the music.*)

GILBERT.

IF YOU'RE PLEASED AS PUNCH WITH WHERE YOU LIVE
AND PROUD OF WHAT YOU DO
YOU'RE ISLAND, YOU'RE ISLAND THROUGH AND THROUGH
AND IF YOU MIND YOUR BUSINESS
AND YOU MIND YOUR NEIGHBOUR'S TOO
YOU'RE ISLAND, YOU'RE ISLAND THROUGH AND THROUGH

ANNE.

IF YOU VOTE THE WAY YOUR FATHER DID
AND HIS OLD MAN BEFORE
IF YOU FEEL A LITTLE ITCHY
WHEN YOU'RE TOO FAR FROM THE SHORE

ANNE & GILBERT.

IF YOU START PREDICTING RAIN
THE MOMENT SKIES ARE TURNING BLUE
YOU'RE ISLAND, YOU'RE ISLAND THROUGH AND THROUGH

YOU'RE ISLAND YOU'RE ISLAND
YOU'RE FROM PRINCE EDWARD ISLAND
YOU'RE ISLAND, YOU'RE ISLAND THROUGH AND THROUGH

YOU'RE ISLAND YOU'RE ISLAND
YOU'RE FROM PRINCE EDWARD ISLAND
YOU'RE ISLAND, YOU'RE ISLAND THROUGH AND THROUGH

JOSIE. *(at* **ANNE***)*

IF YOU HAVE MORE FRECKLES ON YOUR FACE
THAN TURNIPS IN A STEW
YOU'RE ISLAND, YOU'RE ISLAND THROUGH AND THROUGH

MRS. LYNDE. *(pulling* **JOSIE** *away)*

IF YOU DROP IN UNEXPECTEDLY
JUST WHEN THE TEA IS DUE
YOU'RE ISLAND, YOU'RE ISLAND THROUGH AND THROUGH

ANNE & GILBERT.

IF YOU MUCH PREFER THE WAY IT WAS
WHEN IT WAS YESTERDAY
IF YOU'RE JUST A TAD SUSPICIOUS OF PEOPLE FROM AWAY

ANNE.

IF YOU'D SAY NO TO MONTREAL

ALL.

AND YES TO MONTAGUE
YOU'RE ISLAND, YOU'RE ISLAND THROUGH AND THROUGH
YOU'RE ISLAND YOU'RE ISLAND
YOU'RE FROM PRINCE EDWARD ISLAND
YOU'RE ISLAND, YOU'RE ISLAND THROUGH AND THROUGH

YOU'RE ISLAND YOU'RE ISLAND
YOU'RE FROM PRINCE EDWARD ISLAND
YOU'RE ISLAND, YOU'RE ISLAND THROUGH AND THROUGH

(This leads into a big dance, first by **GILBERT** *and then* **ANNE,** *then the rest joining in with a step dance.)*

ALL.

IF SUNDAY FINDS YOU WITH YOUR FAMILY
YAWNING IN THE PEW
YOU'RE ISLAND, YOU'RE ISLAND THROUGH AND THROUGH
IF YOU BELIEVE THAT YOUR FARM
IT HAS THE FINEST VIEW
YOU'RE ISLAND, YOU'RE ISLAND THROUGH AND THROUGH
AND IF YOU THINK THE MAN WHO THINKS HE'S SPECIAL
IS A FOOL
AND SOMEONE TOO AMBITIOUS WILL TASTE YOUR
    RIDICULE
IF YOU DON'T BELIEVE IN GIVING PRAISE
TILL PRAISE IS OVERDUE

YOU'RE ISLAND, YOU'RE ISLAND THROUGH AND THROUGH

YOU'RE ISLAND YOU'RE ISLAND
YOU'RE FROM PRINCE EDWARD ISLAND
YOU'RE ISLAND, YOU'RE ISLAND THROUGH AND THROUGH

YOU'RE ISLAND YOU'RE ISLAND
YOU'RE FROM PRINCE EDWARD ISLAND
YOU'RE ISLAND, YOU'RE ISLAND THROUGH AND THROUGH
YOU'RE ISLAND
YOU'RE ISLAND
YOU'RE ISLAND
YOU'RE ISLAND

(PAUL finally 'gets' the step dance.)

YOU'RE ISLAND THROUGH AND THROUGH

(Everyone leaves except ANNE & MOODY. MOODY, hoping to get her into a romantic mood, plays a little of "All You Can Do Is Wait" on his fiddle. ANNE applauds enthusiastically when he finishes.)

MOODY. Anne! Everyone in town says you're going to end up Mrs. Gilbert Blythe.

ANNE. *(bristling)* NO, I am not!

MOODY. I BELIEVE YOU!

No one else does, but I do!

Prove it, Anne!

ANNE. Prove it? How?

MOODY. By saying you'll be Mrs. Moody Spurgeon MacPherson.

BEFORE YOU SAY NO...

I want you to know that I'm going for the ministry.

ANNE. You?

MOODY. And I'm giving up the fiddle!

ANNE. Oh, don't!

MOODY. It isn't dignified!

I have to be dignified if I'm to be the next minister here in Avonlea!

Think of it, Anne! You, me, and a manse!

ANNE. But, I don't love you, Moody!

MOODY. Oh!

ANNE. I don't love you anymore than I love Gilbert.

MOODY. That's a start!

(rushing off)

I'll write you from Redmond!

ANNE. My first marriage proposal.

A girl only gets ONE first marriage proposal.

Mrs. Moody Spurgeon MacPherson!

*(She grimaces, about to go off when a breathless **DIANA** charges on.)*

DIANA. ANNE! I'M SO GLAD YOU'RE STILL HERE!

ANNE! FRED JUST ASKED ME TO MARRY HIM!

ANNE. AND?

DIANA. AND I SAID 'YES'!

(They jump up and down joyously.)

ANNE. Oh, my dearest of Diana's! When is your wedding date?

DIANA. January! Mum's always promised me an old fashioned Island wedding.

ANNE. Oh, it'll be like a romantic dream. Only colder.

DIANA. And you're going to be my maid of honour, aren't you?

ANNE. Try and stop me!

DIANA. Fred's asking Gil to be his best man.

ANNE. YES! And three-quarters of Avonlea will be saying: 'there's the next wedding'!

DIANA. *(reluctantly)* It's more than three-quarters!

Oh, Anne, I'm so happy!

ANNE.

YOU ARE THE FIRST OF US TO GO
INTO THAT STRANGE MYSTERIOUS PLACE
WHERE MEN AND WOMEN ARE
WHEN NO ONE ELSE IS THERE

NO ONE WILL TELL ME WHAT IT'S LIKE
NO ONE WILL TELL ME WHAT THEY DO
AFTER THE BIG ROMANTIC KISS
IT'S JUST A LITTLE SCARY
I GUESS YOU KNOW

DIANA.

NO, I DON'T

ANNE.

DIANA, SURELY

DIANA.

NO, I DON'T

ANNE.

I THOUGHT, WELL, MADAME
YOU'RE PRACTICALLY A WIFE

DIANA.

I ASKED MY MOTHER, NATURALLY
SHE TURNED AS RED AS RED CAN BE
THEN TOLD ME ALL I'D NEED TO KNOW OF MARRIED LIFE

SHE TALKED ABOUT POLISHING SILVER
AND PUTTING THE SUPPER ON THE TABLE
SHE TALKED ABOUT PUTTING UP PRESERVES HE LIKES
SHE TOLD ME WHAT TO WRITE ON THE LABEL
HOW TO CARE FOR A BABY
HOW TO FIRE A MAID
HOW TO MAKE A PIE THAT'LL MAKE THE GRADE
SHE TALKED ABOUT RAIN
SHE TALKED ABOUT DROUGHT
BUT SHE WOULDN'T SAY WHAT HAPPENS
WHEN YOU BLOW THE CANDLE OUT
WHEN YOU BLOW THE CANDLE OUT

ANNE.

I ASKED MARILLA ONCE, I DID
ABOUT THE SECRETS WOMEN HID
AND SHE REMINDED ME
SHE'D NEVER BEEN A BRIDE
SENT ME TO MRS. LYNDE INSTEAD

DIANA. NO!!!

ANNE.

> WHO TOLD ME;
> 'ALWAYS MAKE YOUR BED
> AND BE SURE YOUR HUSBAND ALWAYS
> SMOKES HIS PIPE OUTSIDE'

ANNE & DIANA.

> THEY TALK ABOUT POLISHING SILVER
> AND DOING THE WASHING ON A MONDAY
> THEY TALK ABOUT IRONING HIS SHIRTS JUST RIGHT
> AND COOKING UP A ROAST EVERY SUNDAY
> HOW TO PLAY THE PIANO
> HOW TO TRAIN A PUP
> AND THE THINGS YOU DO WHEN THE PIPES FREEZE UP
> THEY TELL YOU 'BE DEMURE'
> THEY TELL YOU 'BE DEVOUT'
> BUT THEY NEVER SAY WHAT HAPPENS
> WHEN YOU BLOW THE CANDLE OUT

ANNE.

> I DON'T WANT TO BLOW THE CANDLE OUT

DIANA. Anne, I think it can't be ALL bad. And if you love
him –

ANNE.

> WHEN I WAS A LITTLE GIRL IN FOSTER HOMES
> I USED TO HEAR THE NOISES IN THE NIGHT
> NOT AT ALL ROMANTIC SAD TO SAY
> WHAT YOU HEAR WHEN THE DOORS ARE SHUT UP TIGHT
> THEN IN THE MORNING
> SILENCES
> NO TENDERNESS THAT I COULD SEE
> I DECIDED THEN AND THERE
> PERHAPS THAT LIFE WAS NOT THE LIFE FOR ME
> BUT FOR YOU IT WILL BE DIFFERENT
> DIANA THE PIONEER GODDESS OF LOVE
> GOING WHERE NONE OF US HAS GONE
> YOU MUST FIND OUT WHY SOME MARRIED GIRLS
> GO SMILING THROUGH THE DAY
> WHILE OTHERS LOOK SO VERY PUT UPON

DIANA.

    I'LL TELL YOU 'BOUT POLISHING SILVER

    AND DOING THE WASHING ON A MONDAY

    I'LL TALK ABOUT IRONING HIS SHIRTS JUST RIGHT

ANNE.

    AND COOKING UP A ROAST EVERY SUNDAY

ANNE & DIANA.

    HOW TO PLAY THE PIANO

    HOW TO TRAIN A PUP

    AND THE THINGS YOU DO WHEN THE PIPES FREEZE UP

DIANA.

    I'LL TRY TO BE DEMURE

    I KNOW I'LL BE DEVOUT

    AND I'LL NEVER TELL WHAT HAPPENS

    WHEN YOU BLOW THE CANDLE OUT

    ANNE, I WANT TO BLOW THE CANDLE OUT

ANNE & DIANA.

    WE'LL TALK ABOUT POLISHING SILVER

    (Lights come up on a small beach cove.)

Scene Five

(A small beach cove. To this private spot comes a cheerful **GILBERT**.*)*

GILBERT. *(as he unpacks a towel and books from his knapsack)*
SATURDAY MORNING
I GO TO THE BEACH AND I'M FREED
THE AIR AND THE SURF AND THE SUN
ARE ALL THAT YOU NEED
IF YOU CAN'T HAVE LOVE
IF YOU CAN'T HAVE LOVE
YOU READ
SATURDAY MORNING

SATURDAY MORNING
I GO TO THE BEACH AND I FIND
THE SAND AND THE WAVES AND THE AIR
REFRESHES THE MIND
IF YOU CAN'T HAVE LOVE
IF YOU CAN'T HAVE LOVE
UNWIND
SATURDAY MORNING

I'M TEACHING MONDAY, TUESDAY, WEDNESDAY,
THURSDAY, FRIDAY
AND SATURDAY I TUTOR IN THE AFTERNOON
AND SATURDAY NIGHT I DO
THE SAME THING I DO EVERY OTHER NIGHT
MARKING PAPERS, HELPING OUT AROUND THE HOUSE
ODD JOBS
AN EXTRA ARM
AROUND THE FARM
AND SUNDAY LIKE A FOOL
I TEACH SUNDAY SCHOOL
BUT SATURDAY MORNING

I'VE GOT HIPPOCRATES AND SOCRATES
AND SHAKESPEARE, CERVANTES
AND THOMAS EDISON
AND LOTS OF BOOKS ON MEDICINE

AND LATELY WILLIAM BUTLER YEATS
I'VE GOT THE HISTORY OF BELLS
AND H.G. WELLES' TIME MACHINE WAITS
SATURDAY MORNING

(**GILBERT** *settles down and opens up* The Time Machine. *He barely reads a word, then*)

GILBERT. *(cont.)*

SATURDAY MORNING I GO TO THE BEACH IN THE FALL.
THE SPRAY AND THE WIND AND THE CHILL
I DON'T MIND AT ALL

(Here he starts wading into the icy cold water)

IF YOU CAN'T HAVE LOVE
IF YOU CAN'T HAVE LOVE
IF YOU CAN'T HAVE ANNE. IF YOU CAN'T HAVE ANNE
YOU DO WHAT YOU CAN
IF YOU CAN'T HAVE LOVE LIFE'S GRIM
BUT SATURDAY MORNING
I SWIM

(**GILBERT** *shivers into the water.* **JOSIE PYE,** *with an excited and determined look on her face, steps into the cove and peeks at him. She smiles.*)

JOSIE.

HELLO, GILBERT
HELLO, GIL
I WAS JUST PASSING BY
AWFUL NICE TO FIND YOU
IT'S QUITE THE LITTLE THRILL
TO SEE YOU GIVING ME THE EYE
HELLO, GILBERT, MY OLD PAL
YOU'RE LOOKING PRETTY FIT TODAY
NOTHING GIVES ME JOY
LIKE SEEING MY FAVOURITE BOY
COVERED IN THE SALTY SPRAY

GILBERT. *(V.O. from the back of the hall)*

HELLO, JOSIE, MY OLD FRIEND
WHAT AN UNEXPECTED TREAT
THE WATER'S PRETTY COLD

I WOULDN'T RECOMMEND IT
KEEP YOUR SLIPPERS ON YOUR FEET
NO NO NO
NO NO JOSIE, DON'T COME IN
THE UNDERTOW IS BAD TODAY
JUST THE SLIGHTEST BLUNDER
IT COULD PULL YOU UNDER
BETTER RUN THE OTHER WAY

JOSIE.

HEY, GILBERT, WHATCHA WEARING?
IS YOUR BATHING COSTUME NEW?
SAY IT LOOKS A LITTLE DARING
COME ON OUT AND SHOW ME
I WILL HOLD YOUR TOWEL FOR YOU

GILBERT. *(V.O.)*

LISTEN, JOSIE, YOU'RE JUST GRAND
BUT YOU KNOW I'M SPOKEN FOR
I'M A DESPERATE MAN
BUT IF I CAN'T HAVE ANNE
I'LL BE A BACHELOR FOREVERMORE

JOSIE.

OH, GILBERT. WHY DON'T YOU FACE IT?
SHE DON'T CARE A FIG FOR YOU
YOU'VE A SAD LOOK
I COULD ERASE IT
I'M THE KIND OF GIRL WHO'D DO
WHAT ANNE WOULD NEVER DO

GILBERT. *(pause) (V.O.)*

GO ON, JOSIE
HAVE A HEART
YOU KNOW I'VE HEARD IT ALL BEFORE
SO CLOSE YOUR PRETTY EYES
AND TURN YOUR PRETTY HEAD
AND LET ME COME BACK ON THE SHORE

JOSIE.

AWWW GILBERT

GILBERT. *(V.O.)*

THE LOBSTERS ARE DECLARING WAR

JOSIE.

YOU'LL COME AND SEE ME?

GILBERT. *(V.O.)*

LET ME COME BACK ON THE SHORE

JOSIE. Fine!

*(**JOSIE** storms off taking his clothes and things along for good measure.)*

(Lights dim out, coming up on the graveyard.)

Scene Six

(The graveyard. It is a beautiful moonlit evening. ANNE enters and sits by a tombstone.)

ANNE. Write about myself!

Gilbert, you and your ideas.

(She takes out pad and pencil and begins writing.)

'I was born in Bolingbroke, Nova Scotia. My father's name was Walter Shirley.

(Music begins: "Forever in my Life.")

He was a teacher in the Bolingbroke High School.

My mother's name was Bertha Shirley.

And she taught in the high school too.

And I am a teacher now.

My inheritance, I suppose.

Mrs. Thomas said they were poor as a couple of church mice.

(GILBERT enters. He can't help but listen with interest.)

They went to live in a teeny little yellow house in Bolingbroke.

At 235 Belvedere Lane.

(GILBERT writes down this address.)

I've never seen that house but I have imagined it a thousand times.

I was born in that house.

My mother died of fever when I was three months old.

And my father died four days afterward from fever too.

(The music ends. ANNE looks over what she's done. GILBERT sneezes. Is he catching cold?)

GILBERT. *(since the jig is up anyway)* You're early.

Getting in a little writing?

ANNE. I was just fiddling with an idea. Why did you want to do our Tennyson study here?

GILBERT. Full moon! Bright enough to read by.
Romantic atmosphere.

ANNE. A graveyard?

GILBERT. You know you find graveyards romantic.

ANNE. *(after a stubborn pause)* As a matter of fact, I do.

GILBERT. Uh huh!
And of course, Mr. MacLeod pays me to come here
three times a week to clean up and pull weeds.

ANNE. How many jobs do you have?

GILBERT. *(a moment as he figures it out)* Eight!
If I'm to enter Redmond in the fall, I need every one
of them.
Anyway, nice atmosphere, don't you think?
Who knows, Anne, this might be the night I push my
luck and make the dreaded proposal.

ANNE. You wouldn't dare.

GILBERT. No. Not with you with leaves in your hair, looking
for all the world like a dryad.

ANNE. What a perfect thing to say!

GILBERT. That was good, wasn't it?
Anne, can I tell you a secret, even though it may hurt
my cause?

ANNE. Oh, please do!

GILBERT. I'm going to be a doctor!

ANNE. *(genuinely taken aback)* Why would that hurt your
pathetic and dubious 'cause?'

GILBERT. It means years of medical school before I can get
married.

ANNE. *(with a smile)* My heart is breaking!

*(ANNE suddenly seems very serious. Here is more proof of
what a fine person Gilbert is. She feels guilty for teasing
him.)*

Gilbert, sometimes I don't understand you at all.

(Music begins.)

There isn't a girl in Avonlea who's immune to your charms.

(very quickly)

Except for me.

Why are you waiting for me?

GILBERT.

ALL I CAN DO IS WAIT
ALL I CAN BE IS OPTIMISTIC
ALL I CAN DO IS SIGH
ALL I CAN DO IS TRY
TRY NOT TO TELL YOU
I LOVE YOU
WHEN YOU WALK BY
TRY TO BELIEVE IN FATE
WHEN YOU LOVE SOMEONE LIKE THAT
ALL YOU CAN DO IS WAIT

ALL YOU CAN DO IS KNOW
ALL THAT I KNOW
IS THAT I LOVE YOU
ALL I CAN ASK IS WHY
ALL I CAN DO IS TRY
TRY NOT TO TELL YOU
I LOVE YOU
WHEN YOU WALK BY
TRY NOT TO PALPITATE
WHEN YOU LOVE SOMEONE LIKE THAT
ALL YOU CAN DO IS WAIT

ALL YOU CAN DO IS DREAM
ALL YOU CAN DO IS COUNT THE HOURS
ALL YOU CAN DO IS TRY
TRY NOT SO HARD TO TRY
TRY NOT TO TELL YOU
I LOVE YOU
WHEN YOU WALK BY
TRY TO BELIEVE IN HOPE
WHEN YOU LOVE SOMEONE LIKE THAT
ALL YOU CAN DO IS COPE

WHEN YOU LOVE SOMEONE LIKE THAT
ALL YOU CAN DO IS DREAM
WHEN YOU LOVE SOMEONE LIKE THAT
ALL YOU CAN DO IS WAIT

(After a moment, **ANNE** *suddenly and impulsively kisses* **GILBERT** *on the lips. And it's a long one! Suddenly, she pulls away in horror.)*

ANNE. HOW DARE YOU?

(In a fury, **ANNE** *rushes off.)*

GILBERT. *(with a big smile)*

CARRIED AWAY BY STARS IN THE SKY
CARRIED AWAY BY –

'How dare I?'

(Lights dim out coming up on Green Gables.)

Scene Seven

(Green Gables and then the schoolhouse. **ANNE** *sneezes. Is she catching cold?)*

ANNE.

SOMETHING'S WRONG
OUT OF PLACE
SUCH A THROBBING IN MY FACE
SO MUCH PAIN
SO LITTLE WARNING
I CAN'T GO TO SCHOOL THIS MORNING

MY HEAD IS THROBBING
MY TOOTH IS ACHING
MY ROOM NEEDS TIDYING
MY LIFE NEEDS TIDYING TOO
IT'S NOT LIKE ME TO FEEL THIS WAY
IT'S GONNA BE A JONAH DAY

I BLAME THAT GILBERT. THE FAULT IS GILBERT'S
WHY DID I KISS HIM?
HOW COULD HE HAVE MOVED ME THAT WAY?
I LOST MY HEAD AND I MUST PAY
WITH THIS EVERLASTING JONAH DAY

(Lights come up in the kitchen.)

*(**MARILLA** is preparing breakfast as **MRS. LYNDE** breathlessly enters.)*

MRS. LYNDE. Marilla, I can't stay but a minute.

My Thomas is feeling poorly.

But I thought you'd want to know:

last night, Anne kissed Gilbert!

MARILLA. Where?

MRS. LYNDE. In the cemetery!

MARILLA. ANNE kissed Gilbert?

It wasn't the other way around?

MRS. LYNDE. ANNE kissed Gilbert!

MARILLA. In the cemetery!

How do YOU know?

(ANNE enters the kitchen.)

ANNE. I've often heard it said that if you go into your own room around midnight, lock the door, pull down the blinds and sneeze, the next day Mrs. Lynde will ask you how your cold is!

(Solo spot on ANNE.)

ANNE.

I FEEL SO CRABBY
I FEEL SO CRANKY
THEIR TONGUES ARE WAGGING
AND RACHEL IS WEARING THAT SMARMY SMILE

I WISH THE PUPILS AT AVONLEA SCHOOL
WOULD SMARTEN UP AND MOVE AWAY
'CAUSE THEY'RE IN FOR A JONAH DAY

(Lights come up in the school house.)

(ANNE's PUPILS are in their seats but being particularly noisy.)

ANNE. QUIET!

(The music stops. The PUPILS are shocked at ANNE's outburst. She is not to be reckoned with.)

HOMEWORK!
IN YOUR HANDS
NOW

(The PUPILS quickly comply. ANNE goes from desk to desk appraising their work.)

TERRIBLE!
TERRIBLE!
LAUGHABLE!

(She reaches PAUL.)

HOW SWEET!

ANTHONY PYE. *(mimicking ANNE and taunting PAUL)* How sweet!

(ANNE gets to ANTHONY's homework.)

UNBEARABLE

(She goes on to other desks.)

TERRIBLE!

TERRIBLE!

*(She gets to **JOSIE PYE**'s desk. **ANNE** is stunned.)*

COMPLETE!

*(Spot on **ANNE**.)*

ANNE.

JOSIE PYE HAS DONE HER HOMEWORK
GOD'S TEETH, WHAT A DELIGHT
WHY DO I GET THE FEELING
JOSIE DID IT OUT OF SPITE
MY TEACHER WOULD HAVE PRAISED HER
MISS STACY WOULD HAVE CARED
MISS SHIRLEY JUST GOT CRANKIER
TO FIND THE GIRL PREPARED

JOSIE PYE HAS DONE HER HOMEWORK
GOD'S TEETH, RING THE BELL
PUT UP A BUNCH OF POSTERS
JOSIE'S FINALLY LEARNED TO SPELL
MY TEACHER WOULD HAVE PRAISED HER
MISS STACY WAS ALWAYS RIGHT
MISS SHIRLEY SIMPLY CAN'T BELIEVE
SHE KISSED THOSE LIPS LAST NIGHT

(Lights come back up in the school house.)

*(As a disgruntled **ANNE** goes off for a moment, **JOSIE**, miffed at no praise, leans over to **PAUL**'s desk.)*

JOSIE.

POOR PAUL IRVING
IN HIS LITTLE SUIT
POOR PAUL IRVING
A BRAIN BUT NOT A BRUTE
SO PAUL IRVING
THE BOYS GIVE YOU THE BOOT

JOSIE. *(cont.)*

> AND THEY BOOT YOU TILL YOUR BUM
> LOOKS LIKE MY MUM'S BLACK EYE
> BUT YOU NEVER TELL ANNE SHIRLEY
> AND THAT'S THE REASON WHY
> WHEN I'M STANDING AT YOUR FUNERAL
> I BET I CRY
> POOR PAUL IRVING

Want me to make 'em stop?

PAUL. *(suspicious but nevertheless)* That would be nice.

JOSIE. *(whispering to* **ANTHONY***)* Anthony, lend Paul Napoleon.

ANTHONY. Why?

JOSIE. Paul says he'll put him in Miss Shirley's desk drawer.

ANTHONY. He won't neither!

JOSIE. He will, too!

PAUL. What's Napoleon?

ANTHONY. *(producing 'Napoleon')* My snake.

PAUL. He won't neither!

JOSIE.

> POOR PAUL IRVING

ANNE.

> MY TOOTH IS SCREAMING

ANTHONY. Not a bad idea, though!

> *(***ANTHONY*** skulks toward* **ANNE***'s desk, commando style.)*

ANNE.

> MY SHOES ARE PINCHING

ANTHONY. Come on, Nappy!

> *(***ANTHONY*** skulks further and gets to the desk.* **ANNE** *looks up from the paper she's grading at a student's desk.* **ANTHONY** *ducks behind the desk.)*

ANNE.

> MY CLASSROOM IS UGLY

(**ANTHONY** *puts the snake in the desk drawer.*)

ANNE. *(cont.)*

> AND I FEEL UGLIER STILL
> TONGUE OF METAL
> FEET OF CLAY

> *(During the above,* **ANTHONY** *gets back as* **ANNE** *heads toward her desk.)*

> OH HELP ME MAKE IT THROUGH THIS JONAH DAY

> *(She opens her desk drawer. She screams. She shuts the drawer. After a moment, she picks up her pointer.)*

> Anthony Pye, you are going to get a whooping-WHIP-PING!

PAUL. *(suddenly standing up)* It wasn't Anthony, Teacher. It was me!

ANNE. *(devastated)* NO!

ANTHONY.

> SHE WILL NEVER WHOOP
> NEVER WHOOP
> NEVER WHOOP PAUL IRVING.

> SHE WILL NEVER WHOOP
> NEVER WHOOP
> NEVER WHOOP PAUL IRVING.

ANNE. *(indicating the area by her desk)* Up here, Paul. Now!

ANTHONY & BOYS. *(as* **PAUL** *takes the long walk to the gallows)*

> SHE WILL NEVER WHOOP
> NEVER WHOOP
> NEVER WHOOP PAUL IRVING.

ANTHONY, BOYS & GIRLS.

> SHE WILL NEVER WHOOP
> NEVER WHOOP
> NEVER WHOOP PAUL IRVING.

PAUL. *(joining their chant with)*

> OH LITTLE MOTHER
> UP IN THE SKY
> PROTECT MY REAR
> AND DON'T LET ME CRY

ANNE. *(as they all continue)*
I THOUGHT I COULDN'T

(Add TERRIBLE TERRIBLE for **GIRLS** *and POOR PAUL IRVING for* **JOSIE,** *)*

I SWORE I WOULDN'T
I PROMISED I'D NEVER
HOW SOON THAT PROMISE IS GONE
WHAT WOULD MY OLD TEACHER SAY?
OH WHAT WOULD MY MISS STACY THINK OF ME?

*(***PAUL*** arrives at her desk, indicating to* **ANNE** *that it's alright to go ahead.* **ANNE** *lifts her pointer in the air.)*

TO SINK SO LOW
TO STRIKE A CHILD
TO LOOK SO FOOLISH
TO GET SO RILED
IT'S NOT LIKE ME TO FEEL THIS WAY
I'M TURNING PREMATURELY GREY
OH GOD IT'S SUCH A JONAH.....

(She swats him! The **PUPILS** *all cheer.)*

(Lights change.)

*(***ANNE** *is in a spot outside the schoolhouse. She is beside herself!)*

ANNE. *(melodramatically Anneish)*
I STRUCK THE BEST ONE
I STRUCK THE SWEETEST ONE
I TOOK MY HIGH IDEALS
AND TOSSED THEM AWAY
I LASHED OUT IN ANGER
I ISSUED THE SENTENCE
NO WAY TO BACK DOWN
ON THIS JONAH DAY

AND MY HEART IS BREAKING
MY STANDARDS FALLING
I STAND HERE SHAKING
A MOST DESPICABLE CREATURE
MY TOOTH IS ACHING

MY SHAME IS BURNING
AND I'M NOT WORTHY
OF THE NAME OF TEACHER

(By this time **MARILLA** *has entered. She's seen* **ANNE** *like this before!)*

ANNE. *(cont.)*
WOE! WOE!
WOE IS ME
WOE IS HE
WOE! WOE!
OH GOD, IT'S SUCH A JONAH –

MARILLA. *(interrupting)* Anne, stop this foolishness!
Rachel Lynde's Thomas has passed on.
This is no time for you to feel sorry for yourself.

(Lights dim out coming up on the train station.)

Scene Eight

(The Carmody train station.)

*(**MRS. LYNDE** sits unhappily beside her suitcases, waiting for the train.)*

MRS. LYNDE.
I HAVE A SON IN SUMMERSIDE
WHO'LL GLADLY TAKE ME IN
BUT HE HAS A WIFE
WITH A TONGUE LIKE A KNIFE
AND A SHARP LITTLE POINTY CHIN
OH, THOMAS, WHY'D YOU GO SO SOON?
THERE'S TOO MUCH LEFT UNSAID
YOU'RE NEVER SAFE FROM SURPRISES
TILL YOU'RE....

*(After a moment, **MARILLA** rushes onto the platform.)*

MARILLA. Rachel?

MRS. LYNDE. Don't scold me for not saying goodbye.

I said goodbye to Thomas.

That was as much as I could take.

MARILLA. But why are you leaving, Rachel?

MRS. LYNDE. Thomas and I mortgaged the farm years ago to give Thomas Junior a start in life.

We've never been able to pay much but the interest.

There's nothing left.

I'm going up to Summerside to live with Thomas Junior.

(with great difficulty)

...and his wife!

I'd just as soon live at the bottom of a well as leave Avonlea!

MARILLA. Rachel Lynde, you are the only close friend I've got.

We've been neighbours for 45 years and we've never had a quarrel.

MRS. LYNDE. We came awful near to it the time I called Anne 'homely and red haired', when she first came to you. Remember, Marilla?

MARILLA. You've been family to Anne ever since!

(slight pause)

And you could do something wonderful for her.

MRS. LYNDE. *(suspicious)* More of Anne Shirley's rubbed off on you than the way it was supposed to be!

MARILLA. You know I've never felt right about Anne giving up college to stay home and help me.

But if YOU came to live at Green Gables, I could manage just fine.

You could have the north gable for your bedroom.

And the spare room for your kitchen!

MRS. LYNDE. Kitchen?

MARILLA. The only reason I can think of that two women couldn't get along is if they had to share a kitchen!

MRS. LYNDE. This is just charity, Marilla!

MARILLA. Charity?

RACHEL, YOU KNOW ME BETTER THAN ANYONE

WE'VE BEEN FRIENDS FOR A

CENTURY

YOU KNOW THE PAIN THAT I FEEL AT THE SACRIFICE

DEAR ANNE SHIRLEY HAS MADE FOR ME

AND IT'S HARD FOR ME TO ASK FOR HELP

SO THE ONLY THING THAT I CAN DO

IS REMIND YOU

RACHEL

OF THE WAY WE WERE RAISED

AND THE WORDS YOUR MOTHER OFTEN SAID TO YOU

YOU ALWAYS TOLD ME

WHAT YOUR MOTHER TOLD YOU

THAT HER MOTHER TOLD HER BEFORE

SHE TOLD THE SAME THING TO YOU

THAT SHE'D TELL TO A SON WHO WAS GOING TO WAR

THERE'S SOME DO WELL

THERE'S SOME DO WRONG
AND THE LAGGARDS LOOK FOR BEAUTY
BUT WE PRESBYTERIAN WOMEN KNOW
THAT WHAT WE DO IS OUR DUTY

MARILLA. *(cont.)*

OUR DUTY OUR DUTY
WHAT WE DO IS OUR DUTY
THERE'S WAX ON THE FLOOR
AND THERE'S JAM IN THE PANTRY

MRS. LYNDE.

AND COMPANY HAS TO HAVE TEA
WE DON'T GO TO BED TILL THE DISHES ARE DONE

MARILLA & MRS. LYNDE.

AND WE'VE NO TIME FOR FIDDLE DEE DEE

MARILLA.

AND WHEN WE HEAR A CRY FOR HELP
WE ALWAYS HEED THE CALL
WE PRESBYTERIAN WOMEN PUT OUR DUTY OVER ALL

MARILLA & MRS. LYNDE.

OUR DUTY OUR DUTY
OUR DUTY OVER ALL

MARILLA.

THOMAS WOULD WANT YOU TO STAY IN AVONLEA
THOMAS WOULD SURELY UNDERSTAND
I CAN HEAR HIM SAYING;
'STOP YOUR BLETHERING, RACHEL
AND GO GIVE MARILLA A HAND'
YOU ALWAYS SAID THAT THE CHURCH WAS IMPORTANT BUT

MARILLA & MRS. LYNDE.

NEIGHBOURLINESS IS THE CORE'

MARILLA.

WE STICK TOGETHER
WE DO FOR EACH OTHER

MARILLA & MRS. LYNDE.

CUZ THAT'S WHAT OLD FRIENDS ARE FOR

MARILLA.

YOU'D BE MY EYES WHEN LIGHTS ARE DIM

MRS. LYNDE.

I AM GOOD COMPANY

MARILLA & MRS. LYNDE.

WE PRESBYTERIAN WOMEN FIND
THERE'S STRENGTH IN UNITY
OUR DUTY OUR DUTY
WHAT WE DO IS OUR DUTY
OUR DUTY OUR DUTY
SAVED
BY OUR SENSE OF DUTY

MRS. LYNDE.

MARILLA, YOU KNOW THERE'S ONE THING MORE
MY SAINTED MOTHER SAID:

(as **MARILLA** *mouths the words)*

'YOU'RE NEVER SAFE FROM SURPRISES
'TILL YOU'RE DEAD'

(Lights dim out coming up on the schoolhouse exterior.)

Scene Nine

(Outside the schoolhouse.)

(The last of **ANNE**'s **PUPILS** *are leaving for the day. The weather is turning colder.* **ANNE** *steps outside.* **JOSIE** *rushes out.)*

ANNE. Josie?

JOSIE. *('What have I done now?')* Yes, Miss Shirley?

ANNE. I've been meaning to talk to you about your work.

JOSIE. What's wrong with it now?

ANNE. It's been excellent.

If you keep it up you're certain to graduate this year.
And I was wondering if you'd be interested in a recommendation to attend teachers' college?

JOSIE. You would recommend me?

ANNE. Even as your classmate, I always suspected that the day you stopped flirting and cracked a book, you'd be as gifted a scholar as anyone in Avonlea.

JOSIE. *(genuinely astonished)* I didn't.

I'd very much like your recommendation, Miss Shirley.

ANNE. I think you can call me 'Anne' when no one's listening.

JOSIE. Not till I graduate, Miss Shirley.

(She smiles and runs out. **PAUL** *rushes on carrying a brand new pair of ice skates.)*

ANNE. Paul, I need a word with you!

PAUL. I'm sorry, Miss Shirley, the pond's finally frozen over and they've asked me to play hockey.

ANNE. But you're from America!

Have you ever played hockey?

PAUL. I've been reading up on it.

ANNE. Can you skate?

PAUL. I've been reading up on it.

ANNE. Paul –

PAUL. And practicing on my new skates in Grandmother's barn.

ANNE. *(an understatement)* This is not a good idea, Paul.

PAUL. But, Miss Shirley, since you whooped me –

ANNE. 'Whipped!'

PAUL. They like me!

Miss Shirley, you don't know how grateful I am for the whipping!

It changed my life!

I'm sorry, Miss Shirley, they're waiting for me!

ANNE. Paul, you are going to have to believe me, you are NOT ready for hockey!

(MARILLA comes up the path.)

Marilla, what are you doing here?

PAUL. Goodbye, Miss Shirley!

(He runs off.)

ANNE. PAUL, YOU STAY OFF THE ICE! This is all my fault!

MARILLA. I was expecting Diana.

I wanted her here to help me with this.

Anne, I suppose with Gilbert Blythe going to university in the fall, you'd like to go too.

ANNE. *(This is the last thing she expected to hear.)* It has nothing to do with Gilbert. I'd like to go, of course, but it isn't possible this year.

MARILLA. I guess it can be made possible. I've always felt you should go and I never felt right about you giving it up on my account.

Your salary from teaching ought to cover a year of accommodation and –

ANNE. I'm not leaving you alone and that's final! I know your eyesight is better, but –

MARILLA. Rachel Lynde is moving into the north gable.

She can't afford to stay in Avonlea on her own and I thought if she could help me, you could go to Redmond.

ANNE. Marilla, what a wonderful idea!

Oh, but it still wouldn't be enough. AND YOU ARE
NOT TOUCHING YOUR SAVINGS!

MARILLA. *(spotting* **DIANA,** *relieved)* We won't have to. DIANA!

DIANA. You didn't tell her did you?

MARILLA. Only that she's going to university. YOU tell her
why.

DIANA. Oh, Anne! I'm just full of surprises for you!

First off, my Aunt Josephine died.

ANNE. I knew that!

DIANA. She mentioned you in her will.

ANNE. Why would she do that?

DIANA. Anne, are you forgetting? Every year when she came
to visit – for a month! – you spent more time with her
than anyone that HAD to!

ANNE. I genuinely liked the dear old lady.

DIANA. *(still amazed)* I know.

None of our family ever did.

But that's what makes this so perfect.

Anne, she's left you your tuition. All four years at Redmond.

ANNE. *(moved)* I don't believe it.

DIANA. But that's not even the best surprise!

Anne, you have won the Rollings Reliable Baking
Powder Literary Competition!

ANNE. I didn't enter!

DIANA. I entered for you!

You gave 'Averil's Ideal' to me.

I wasn't going to say anything if you didn't win so you
wouldn't feel bad.

But you did win, Anne!

It's not as much as tuition of course.

But it could be enough for a big city outfit.

Or six.

Anne, you don't seem a bit pleased!

ANNE. There wasn't a word in my story about baking powder!

DIANA. Oh, I put that in. It was easy as a wink.

NOW AVERIL NEVER MADE MISTAKES
WHEN SHE WHIPPED UP HER HONEY CAKES
ROLLINGS RELIABLE BAKING POWDER
ENSURED HER GREAT SUCCESS
ONE RAINY NIGHT SHE MET A MAN
AND GAVE HIM ONE HOT FROM THE PAN
HE FELL IN LOVE AND SOON SHE WORE
A LONG WHITE WEDDING DRESS
NEVER A BRIDE SO GAY
ROLLINGS SAVED THE DAY

THERE HAD TO BE A TREE
THERE HAD TO BE SOME CAKE
CUZ HEROES ALWAYS LONG FOR
A LADY WHO CAN BAKE
AND SHE HAD FOUND HER DREAM
A GENTLEMAN GENTEEL
RELIABLE AS ROLLINGS
WAS AVERIL'S IDEAL

Congratulations, Anne.
I'M GOING TO MISS YOU SO MUCH!
Of course, I am getting married next month!
Bye!

(She rushes off.)

ANNE. I'm going to Redmond! Oh, Marilla!
SOMEONE HANDED ME THE MOON TODAY
I'VE BEEN GLAD BEFORE BUT THIS IS MORE THAN
    GLORIOUS
SOMEONE HAS ARRANGED FOR ME TO FEEL VICTORIOUS
ALL MY DREAMS ARE COMING TRUE SO SOON
SOMEONE HANDED ME THE MOON

*(**MARILLA** goes off.)*

ANNE. *(cont.)*
ALL MY DEAREST FRIENDS HAVE RALLIED 'ROUND

BRINGING ME GOOD FORTUNE WHEN I WASN'T LOOKING
I CAN'T BELIEVE THE SCHEMES THAT THEY WERE
   'COOKING'
FEEL LIKE I COULD DANCE IN A SALOON
SOMEONE HANDED ME THE MOON

AND OH, IT'S SO FULL AND SHINY WHITE
I PROMISE I WILL PUT IT BACK BEFORE TONIGHT
ROLL IT UP THE SKY LIKE A WAGON WHEEL
FOR THE LIGHT THAT IT SHEDS
IS THE LIGHT OF THE LOVE I FEEL

SOMEONE HANDED ME THE MOON TODAY
SOMEONE GAVE ME WATER JUST WHEN I WAS THIRSTING
MY JOY'S COMPLETE, OH HOW MY HEART IS BURSTING
LIKE A TODDLER ROLLING DOWN THE DUNE
SOMEONE HANDED ME THE MOON
SOMEONE HANDED ME THE MOON

(Lights dim out.)

Scene Eleven

(Outside the wedding.)

*(First **MOODY SPURGEON MACPHERSON** enters carrying his fiddle.)*

MOODY. I come all the way home from Redmond for this wedding and what do I get?
"DON'T FORGET YOUR FIDDLE, MOODY!"

*(He stomps off. **PAUL IRVING** enters on crutches, his leg broken. The **GUESTS** are assembled and the wedding has begun. An exceedingly nervous **FRED** comes on with his best man, **GILBERT**. **ANNE**, the maid of honour, enters, followed by the radiant bride, **DIANA**.)*

ALL. *(except for **DIANA** & **FRED**)*

BLESSED BE THE AVONLEA BRIDE
WITH HER BRIDEGROOM BY HER SIDE
BLESSED BE THE HYMNS WE SING
LASTING BE THE JOY THEY BRING

BELLS RING OUT ALL OVER THE LAND
AS HE SWEETLY TAKES HER HAND
MAY THEIR LOVE BE STRONG AND TRUE
'TIL THEIR TIME ON EARTH IS THROUGH

LORD ABOVE THESE THINGS WE PRAY
BLESS THE HAPPY PAIR TODAY
MAY THEY ALWAYS SING THY PRAISE
SEND THEM LITTLE ONES TO LIGHT THEIR DAYS

THE MINISTER.

BLESSED BE THE AVONLEA BRIDE

*(By the end of the hymn, the wedding ceremony has been mimed. **FRED** & **DIANA** kiss. **MOODY** starts to play. **FRED** takes **DIANA** in his arms and they start to waltz.)*

ANNE & GILBERT.

LOOK AT YOU SMILING
EVER SO HAPPY
NEVER SO GLAD
EVER IN YOUR LIFE

PICTURE OF WEDDED BLISS
WHAT COULD BE FINER THAN THIS?
CARRIED AWAY BY LOVE

ANNE & GILBERT. *(cont.)*

YOU HAVE YOUR SOMEONE
SOMEONE TO LEAN ON
SOMEONE TO LOVE
SOMEONE WHO LOVES YOU
SOMEONE TO HOLD YOU DEAR
YEAR AFTER YEAR AFTER YEAR
CARRIED AWAY BY LOVE

SHARING A HOME
AND SHARING A NAME
THERE BY YOUR SIDE SHE'LL STAY
LOVE THAT WILL BURN
WITH STEADIEST FLAME
FEET ON THE GROUND
YOU'VE FOUND YOU'VE BEEN CARRIED AWAY

*(**FRED & DIANA** and their **GUESTS** go off. **GILBERT** tries to take **ANNE**'s hand.)*

ANNE. Gilbert, what are you doing?

GILBERT. Anne, there is something I have to ask you.

ANNE. *(after the realization of what's about to happen)* Don't say it Gilbert! Please don't say it.

GILBERT. Things have gone on like this long enough!
Anne, I love you. You know I do.
I-I can't tell you how much.
Will you promise me that one day you'll be my wife?

ANNE. I can't. Oh, Gilbert, you've spoiled everything.

GILBERT. Don't you care for me at all?

ANNE. Not in that way.
I do care a great deal for you as a friend.
But I don't love you, Gilbert.

GILBERT. But can't you give me some hope that you will – yet?

ANNE. No I can't. I can never love you in that way.
You must never speak of this to me again.

(After a moment, **GILBERT** *hands her his gold piece.
Then he goes off.)*

ANNE. *(looking sadly at the gold piece)*
I'M NOT THE KIND WHO COULD BE
CARRIED AWAY BY LOVE

(The first act curtain falls.)

ACT TWO

Scene One

(Before the curtain rises, a **PROFESSOR** *solemnly faces the audience.)*

PROFESSOR. Ladies and gentlemen, I give you, the freshman class!

(The curtain rises on the freshman class at Redmond. **ANNE & GILBERT** *are among them. They are in a stately pose, as though for a class picture.)*

ALL.

REDMOND, OH REDMOND
EVER TO THEE
SCENIC AND STALWART UNIVERSITY
REDMOND, OH REDMOND
TIMELESS AS THE SEA
I'M FAITHFUL REDMOND
EVER TO THEE
EVER TO REDMOND
EVER TO THEE

(The music changes and all is chaos.)

THE DAYS AHEAD ARE FILLED
WITH PEOPLE, BRILLIANT PEOPLE
NOT AT ALL LIKE ME
I FEEL SO ALONE

GIRL.

I COME FROM SHEDIAC

BOY.

ST. JOHN'S

ROYAL GARDNER.

> I'M FROM TORONTO
> AND I'M NOT IMPRESSED
> IF ONLY I HAD KNOWN

ALL.

> I SHOULD BE THRILLED TO BE IN COLLEGE
> FOR WISDOM, FOR KNOWLEDGE
> FOR A REDMOND RESUME
> I WANT MY MOTHER

ANNE.

> AND I WANT MARILLA

ALL.

> I'D RATHER RUN AWAY
> THAN FACE THIS DAY

ANNE.

> REDMOND, OH REDMOND
> NOW THAT I'M HERE
> CAN I SURVIVE THIS URBAN ATMOSPHERE?
> REDMOND, OH REDMOND
> AWFUL AND AUSTERE
> HOW WILL I EVER LIVE THROUGH MY FRESHMAN YEAR?

(A female **TRIO** *of sophomores, obviously popular girls on campus, enter the scene and dish the newcomers)*

TRIO.

> FRESHETTES, FRESHETTES
> TAKE A LOOK AT THE FRESHETTES
> THE NEW FRESHETTES
> ARE SUCH TRUE FRESHETTES
> THEY DON'T KNOW WHAT THEY ARE OR WHERE TO GO
>
> SO GREEN! SO GREEN!
> THEY'RE THE GREENEST EVER SEEN
> THE CROP THIS YEAR
> IS A FLOP THIS YEAR
> OH WHEN DID REDMOND'S STANDARDS SINK SO LOW?
>
> FRESHETTES, FRESHETTES
> BACK WHEN WE WERE THE FRESHETTES
> WE WERE FABULOUS FRESHETTES

NO PLAIN JANES
NOT LIKE THOSE
WE HAD BRAINS
WE HAD CLOTHES
WE WERE THE CREAM OF THE CROP OF THE CLASS
WE HUFFED AND WE PUFFED
AND WE BLEW DOWN THE DOORS
WE HAD THE STYLE
HAD THE FLAIR
HAD THE SASS
WE WERE AS CHIC AS THE CHIC SOPHOMORES
THESE GIRLS LOOK LIKE LABRADORS

TRIO. *(cont.)*

FRESHETTES, FRESHETTES
EVEN FABULOUS FRESHETTES
LIKE LAST YEAR'S FRESHETTES
HAD SOPHOMORES WHO MADE THEM PAY
BELITTLED THEM IN EVERY WAY
WE'RE GLAD WE'RE NOT YOU
FRESHETTES TODAY

ANNE. *(As* **ANNE** *sings this,* **ALEX & ALONZO** *rush by her. Apparently these young men about campus are in pursuit of someone.)*

HOMESICK, I'M HOMESICK
I DON'T LIKE THE PACE
FRANTIC AND FRIGHTENING
I DON'T LIKE THE PLACE
'ANNE OF GREEN GABLES'
GONE WITHOUT A TRACE
I WOULD DIE JUST TO SEE ONE FAMILIAR FACE

("Saturday Morning" plays as **GILBERT** *walks by. He and* **ANNE** *see each other. The music stops. There is an extremely uncomfortable moment.* **ANNE** *gives him an uncomfortable wave before she rushes off. Music begins again as* **GILBERT** *tries to concern himself with other matters.)*

GILBERT.

> SATURDAY MORNING
> I'M RAKING THE CITADEL LAWN
> AND THEN I SELL PROGRAMS AT
> 'AFTERNOON OF A FAUN'
> AND FOUR DAYS A WEEK DELIVERING FLOWERS
> AND TUTORING GREEK FOR SIX OR SO HOURS
> IN CHARLOTTE'S CAFE
> WHERE POSH STUDENTS MEET
> I MEET A TRAY
> EVEN ON SUNDAY

> *(MOODY enters and spots GILBERT.)*

MOODY. GIL!

GILBERT. MOODY SPURGEON MACPHERSON.

I almost didn't recognize you without your fiddle.

MOODY. I've given the fiddle up for the ministry.

GILBERT. *(surprised)* All right.

MOODY. Seen Anne?

> *(Pause, GILBERT's humorous mood evaporates.)*

Sorry, Gil. Haven't you finally given up on her?
I have.

GILBERT. I will never propose marriage to her again.

She's going to have to propose to me!

MOODY. And they say I'm crazy.

> *(MOODY follows GILBERT off. Suddenly the beautiful young PHILIPPA GORDON, noticeably better dressed than the other girls, rushes on. It is she being pursued by ALEC & ALONZO. She takes the time to take a good look at GILBERT as he rushes off. But then she concentrates on avoiding her young pursuers, who are hot on her trail. PHIL seems to be very much enjoying the chase. The TRIO of sophomores is quite impressed.)*

TRIO.

> THAT GIRL, THAT GIRL
> THAT'S THE YOUNGEST GORDON GIRL

THE FINEST STOCK
THAT'S A PARIS FROCK
HER DAD ENDOWED THIS UNIVERSITY

PHIL.

HERE COME THOSE BEAUX AGAIN
UH OH THOSE BEAUX AGAIN
SO ATTRACTIVE
BUT SO DOOMED TO FAIL

I PROMISED FAITHFULLY
'DAD,' I SAID FAITHFULLY
'I WILL MAKE AT LEAST ONE FRIEND WHO'S
FEMALE'

TRIO.

THE PEARLS, THE PEARLS
OYSTERS DIED TO MAKE THOSE PEARLS
THAT'S ONE FRESHETTE
YOU WILL NOT FORGET
SHE'S FRESHER THAN A FRESHETTE OUGHT TO BE

PHIL. *(looking at the* **TRIO***)*

I WON'T BE ONE OF THEM
PLEASE GOD, NOT ONE OF THEM
SOME PRETENCE OF REASON MUST PREVAIL

HERE COME THOSE BEAUX AGAIN
UH OH THOSE BEAUX AGAIN
TIME FOR LITTLE PHILIPPA TO SET SAIL

*(***PHIL** *is chased off by* **ALEC & ALONZO**. **ANNE** *re-enters, holding a letter and is quite cheered.)*

ANNE.

I GOT A LETTER
A LETTER FROM HOME
HERE TO REMIND ME:
ANNE, ALTHOUGH YOU ROAM
OUR LOVE IS STEADY AS A METRONOME
WE ARE THERE WITH YOU ON EVERY BEACH YOU COMB

*(***ANNE** *repeats the above counterpoint to the rest of the* **STUDENTS** *singing the Redmond anthem. Then* **GIL-BERT** *comes back.)*

GILBERT.

> THE DAY AHEAD'S
> A DAY I'VE READ ABOUT
> I'VE DREAMT ABOUT
> I'VE STUDIED FOR
> MY FIRST DAY BACK TO SCHOOL
> BUT NOT THE TEACHER ANYMORE
> AND NOT THE ONE AND ONLY MAN FOR ANNE
> THERE MUST BE MEN GALORE
> THAT SHE'LL IGNORE

ANNE.

> THE DAYS AHEAD
> ARE DAYS AWAY
> AND YET I FEEL ALREADY
> DAYS BEHIND
> SO ASK ME IF I CARE
> I'M NOT THE TEACHER ANY MORE
> I'M NOT THE ONE AND ONLY GIRL IN TOWN
> WHO'S FAMOUS FOR HER FRECKLES, FOR HER FOIBLES
> FOR HER GABLES
> FOR HER HAIR

GILBERT.

> SHE'LL TOSS THEIR BROKEN HEARTS INTO THE AIR

ANNE.

> AND THAT IS WHY THE BELLS ARE RINGING

ANNE & GILBERT.

> AND REDMOND IS SINGING
> AND THE SUN THAT SHINES TODAY
> WILL SHINE TOMORROW
> YOUR CHOSEN TOMORROW
> WHERE YOU'LL SUCCEED SOMEHOW
> IT STARTS RIGHT NOW

ALL STUDENTS.

> THE DAYS AHEAD
> ARE DAYS I WISH I DIDN'T DREAD
> SEE I'M THE KIND THAT CRAMS
> TWO DAYS BEFORE EXAMS
> I HOPE THAT ONE DAY I'LL BE WISE

BEFORE I'M DEAD
I HOPE PROFESSORS PRIZE
THE PITHY THINGS I'VE SAID

ALL STUDENTS. *(cont.)*

AND THAT IS WHY THE BELLS ARE RINGING
AND REDMOND IS SINGING
AND THE SUN THAT SHINES TODAY
WILL SHINE TOMORROW
OUR CHOSEN TOMORROW
WHERE WE'LL SUCCEED SOMEHOW
WE START RIGHT NOW

(REDMOND, OH REDMOND, EVER TO THEE)
WE START RIGHT NOW
(REDMOND, OH REDMOND, EVER TO THEE)
WE START RIGHT NOW
(REDMOND, OH REDMOND, TIMELESS AS THE SEA)
WE START RIGHT NOW

(As lights dim out on this scene, **ANNE** *walks directly into Old St. John's Cemetery.)*

Scene Two

(Old St. John's Cemetery.)

(ANNE settles comfortably and takes a letter from her bag. PHIL rushes on. She looks behind her to make sure she's lost the two men who've been following her.)

PHIL. *(quite pleased with herself)* Lost 'em!

(All of this has not gone unnoticed by ANNE, who seems awfully amused. PHIL spots ANNE.)

Oh! It's you! I've been longing to meet you.

ANNE. Me? Why?

PHIL. Well, I'm obviously the richest girl on campus.

ANNE. Obviously!

PHIL. And you're the poorest.

ANNE. Obviously?

PHIL. *(offering her hand)* Philippa Gordon!

ANNE. *(shyly)* Oh my! Your reputation precedes you.

PHIL. Does it ever!

Do call me Phil right off! Now what's your handle?

ANNE. *(smiling and shaking her hand)* Anne Shirley. I'm from Prince Edward Island.

PHIL. As you probably know, I hail from Bolingbroke, Nova Scotia.

ANNE. That's where I was born. I've always wanted to go back there.

PHIL. Whatever for? The only fun in that town is me and I'm here!

ANNE. I want to see the house I was born in, see if I can find out anything about my parents.

They died when I was an infant and I really don't know much about them.

PHIL. I know too much about my family.

Daddy & my brothers were dead set against my going to university.

Somehow they got the idea that I'm boy mad.

But then when I won top of the class, senior year…

ANNE. What could Daddy do?

PHIL. Well, exactly!

Say, did you happen to notice the two boys who've been hound-dogging me all day?

ANNE. They were hard to miss!

PHIL. Not fortune hunters, mind you! Both from top-notch families!

ANNE. Well, I should hope so!

PHIL. *(a bit surprised)* Are you laughing at me?

ANNE. Ummm hmmm!

PHIL. *(after a moment, genuinely delighted)* Well, good!

The Boys followed me all the way from home!

Enrolled at Redmond and everything!

ANNE. Do you love either of them?

PHIL. I couldn't love anybody! It isn't in me.

ANNE. *(surprised that this conversation has taken such a serious turn)* Do you really mean that?

Sometimes I wonder about that in myself.

PHIL. Being in love makes you a perfect slave, I think!

(sentimentally)

I look at my mum and dad and I say;

(defiantly)

NO!

(She smiles.)

BOYS COME BY AND WON'T GO AWAY
WHAT'S A GIRL SUPPOSED TO SAY?
WHAT IF SHE'S NOT READY YET TO CHOOSE?

HOW THEY CRY AND HOW THEY FUSS
HOW THEY PLACE THE BLAME ON US
BUT TAKE AWAY THEIR BALANCE AND THEY LOSE

I SUPPOSE I'M A SEESAW GIRL
HEAVEN KNOWS I'M A SEESAW GIRL
SO I TEETER TOTTER UP AND DOWN
I SINK
I FLY

PHIL. *(cont.)*

    WHAT'S THE ROLE OF A SEESAW GIRL?
    WHAT'S GOAL OF A SEESAW GIRL?
    BALANCING THE BOYS THROUGH SLIGHT OF MIND
    I'M CRUEL
    I'M KIND
    I'M WISE
    I'M BLIND
    ALEC AND ALONZO
    THEY WORSHIP ME, THEY WOO
    THEY'RE FAITHFUL AND THEY'RE LOYAL
    THEY STICK TO ME LIKE GLUE
    THEY FOLLOWED ME TO SCHOOL ONE DAY
    SO WHAT'S A GIRL TO DO?
    WITH FOUR EYES THAT YEARN
    AND TWO HEARTS THAT BURN
    FOR THE SEESAW GIRL

    (**ALEC & ALONZO** *jump out from behind a tombstone.*)

PHIL.

    I SUPPOSE I'M A SEESAW GIRL

ALEC & ALONZO.

    I SUPPOSE SHE'S A SEESAW GIRL

PHIL.

    HEAVEN KNOWS I'M A SEESAW GIRL

ALEC & ALONZO.

    HEAVEN KNOWS SHE'S A SEESAW GIRL

PHIL.

    SO I TEETER TOTTER UP AND DOWN

ALEC & ALONZO.

    SO SHE TEETER TOTTERS UP AND DOWN

PHIL.

    I SINK

ALEC & ALONZO.

    SO LOW

PHIL.

    I FLY

ALEC & ALONZO.

SO HIGH
WE GO APE FOR THE SEESAW GIRL
STAY IN SHAPE FOR THE SEESAW GIRL
EVERYWHERE SHE GOES WE'RE RIGHT BEHIND

PHIL.

I'M CRUEL

ALEC & ALONZO.

SO CRUEL

PHIL.

I'M KIND

ALEC & ALONZO.

SO KIND

PHIL.

I'M WISE

ALEC & ALONZO.

SO WISE

PHIL.

I'M BLIND

ALEC & ALONZO.

SO BLIND

ALL THREE.

ALEC AND ALONZO

PHIL.

THEY WORSHIP ME, THEY WOO

ALEC & ALONZO. *(lustily)*

WOO WOO

PHIL.

THEY'RE FAITHFUL AND THEY'RE LOYAL

ALEC & ALONZO.

WE STICK TO HER LIKE GLUE
WE FOLLOWED HER TO SCHOOL ONE DAY

PHIL.

THEY'LL STAY UNTIL I'M THROUGH

ALL THREE.
>WITH FOUR EYES THAT YEARN
>AND TWO HEARTS THAT BURN

PHIL.
>FOR THE SEESAW GIRL

ALEC & ALONZO.
>FOR THE SEESAW GIRL

PHIL.
>FOR THE SEESAW GIRL

ALEC & ALONZO.
>FOR THE SEESAW GIRL

PHIL.
>FOR THE SEESAW GIRL

ALEC & ALONZO.
>FOR THE SEESAW GIRL

PHIL.
>FOR THE SEESAW GIRL

ALEC & ALONZO.
>FOR THE SEESAW GIRL

ALL THREE.
>FOR THE SEESAW GIRL
>FOR THE SEESAW GIRL

PHIL. SHOO!

>*(ALEC & ALONZO rush off.)*

ANNE. I can't believe you get away with that!

PHIL. They do worship me!

>But I'm not going to let that stop ME from having a good time at Redmond.
>
>I expect to have heaps of beaux.
>
>I can't be happy if I don't.
>
>But don't you think the freshmen are fearfully homely?
>
>I've only spotted one really handsome fellow in the whole lot!
>
>I heard a chum call him Gilbert...Smythe, I think!

ANNE. Blythe, I think.

PHIL. Uh oh! Yours?

ANNE. Well, he did propose.

But I said 'no!'

PHIL. Really?

Good for you!

But I'll keep my mittens off that one!

Just in case.

Boys naturally adore me.

ANNE. Naturally!

PHIL. Somehow, girls never do!

Not girls who are worthwhile.

But you do, just a little bit! Now, don't you?

ANNE. You know, Phil, we are surprisingly kindred spirits!

PHIL. Good! Then we'll see lots of each other. Got to run now.

Come on, boys!

(ALEC & ALONZO pop out from behind another tombstone and follow PHIL off. ANNE smiles in amazement. She sits back down to read her letter.)

ANNE. *(reading)* 'Dear Anne, the weather's been fine since you left.'

(Lights come up on MARILLA.)

MARILLA. Not a trace of frost in the milking pail.

I have to say, I'm glad Rachel's here.

Who'd have thought we would get along so well?

Anne, there's something I've been holding back.

A very old tale I think it's time to tell.

I'M NOT ONE TO GIVE ADVICE ABOUT
MATTERS OF THE HEART
BUT WHEN I THINK OF YOU AND GILBERT
AN OLD WOUND BEGINS TO SMART

ONCE UPON A TIME
I WAS YOUNG LIKE YOU
HARD FOR YOU TO PICTURE

ME THE INGENUE
AND THERE WAS A MAN
AND I MADE HIM GO
LIFE WAS SO MUCH SWEETER
WHEN HE WAS MY BEAU

MARILLA. *(cont.)*

WE HAD BITTER WORDS
I FORGET WHAT FOR
I WAS FULL OF PRIDE THEN
I SHOWED HIM TO THE DOOR
AND OH MY TONGUE WAS SHARP
AND I HURT HIM SO
ALL MY LIFE I'VE WISHED THAT
HE WERE STILL MY BEAU

OPEN UP YOUR EYES
AND SEE THE MAN WHO'S WAITED
OPEN UP YOUR HEART
HE LOVES YOU, HE'S YOUR FRIEND
WHAT I HAVE TO SAY MAY BE DUSTY
PERHAPS IT'S DATED
STUBBORNESS CAN LEAD TO A BAD BAD END

DON'T MAKE MY MISTAKE
DON'T LET HIM SLIP AWAY
WHEN HE WEDS ANOTHER
YOUR HEART WILL PAY AND PAY
EVERYBODY SEES
SURELY YOU MUST KNOW
YOU'RE MEANT TO BE TOGETHER
HE'S MEANT TO BE YOUR BEAU
FOR LOVE THAT'S TURNED ASIDE
CAN MELT LIKE FALLEN SNOW
I THINK HE'S DESTINED FOR YOU
BORN TO BE YOUR BEAU

(ANNE puts the letter back into her bag. There is a sudden crack of thunder. ANNE looks up at the heavens.)

What else must I endure?

(ANNE rushes for the nearest tree.)

Scene Three

(Underneath a tree outside the cemetery.)

(ANNE ducks underneath it and promptly spots a dream come true. The "Averil's Ideal" theme plays as ANNE tries not to stare at the handsome young man with the umbrella. The handsome young man with the umbrella takes note of ANNE.)

ROY.

PARDON ME MISS
FORGIVE MY BOLDNESS
BUT I SEE THAT YOU ARE NOT THE LEAST PREPARED
FOR THE DOWNPOUR
IT'S QUITE A DOWNPOUR
AND HERE WE ARE
MAY I OFFER MY UMBRELLA?
MAY I OFFER MY UMBRELLA?

PARDON ME, MISS
YOU LOOK FAMILIAR
DID I SEE YOU ONE DAY LAUGHING WITH YOUR FRIENDS
ON THE CAMPUS?
NO, NOT THE CAMPUS
IT COULDN'T BE
HOW COULD A SCHOLAR LOOK SO LOVELY?
HOW COULD A SCHOLAR LOOK SO LOVELY?

IT SEEMS TO ME THAT YOUR EYES ARE LIKE STARLIGHT
I'M NOT A POET BUT YOUR EYES ARE LIKE STARLIGHT
YOUR SMILE IS HEAVEN
AND YOUR EYES ARE LIKE STARLIGHT
OH YOU MUST THINK ME SUCH AN ILL-MANNERED MAN!
MY NAME IS ROY

ANNE.

MY NAME IS ANNE

ROY.

ANNE WITH AN E?

ANNE.

DEFINITELY

ROY.

> PARDON ME, MISS
> I HAVE A QUESTION
> DO YOU COME HERE OFTEN?
> MAY I HAVE THIS DANCE?
> WHAT A NICE FLOOR
> IT'S SUCH A NICE FLOOR
> AND HERE WE ARE
> I FEEL I'VE KNOWN YOU FOR A LONG TIME
> I'VE KNOWN YOU SUCH A LONG TIME
> MAY I WALK YOU TO YOUR DOOR?
>
> *(***ROY*** lifts his umbrella. ***ANNE*** gets under it. He offers his arm. She takes it. They go off together.)*
>
> *(Lights dim out coming up on AVONLEA.)*

Scene Four

(Avonlea)

*(A very pregnant **DIANA** is helped into her easy chair by her loving husband **FRED**. **DIANA** can't wait to read the letter she's opening.)*

DIANA. *(reading it)* 'Dearest of Dianas';
I love it when she calls me that!

'I HAVE KNOWN ROY THREE WEEKS NOW
I CAN'T FIND A SINGLE FLAW
HOW HE LOOKS
HOW HE SPEAKS
HOW HE QUOTES HIS BERNARD SHAW'

FRED. Who?

DIANA.

'AND I LOVE THE WAY HE KISSES
AND I LOVE THE WAY HE CRIES

FRED. He cries?

DIANA.

AND GILBERT WOULD NEVER COMPOSE
A SONNET TO MY EYES'

FRED. No, I don't think he would!

*(**FRED**'s had enough. He goes off.)*

DIANA.

'ROY IS BRAVE AND ROMANTIC
WHEN HE TALKS ABOUT HIS DREAMS
BY THE WAY DID I MENTION;
HE'S A MILLIONAIRE IT SEEMS'

*(The baby apparently kicks! **DIANA** looks at her bundle of joy.)*

Calm down, Little Anne!

'AND I REALLY LIKE HIS SHOULDERS
AND I EVEN LIKE HIS TIES
AND GILBERT WOULD NEVER COMPOSE

A SONNET TO MY EYES

(**ANNE** *appears.*)

DIANA & ANNE.

GILBERT WOULD NEVER COMPOSE
HE HAS NO PATIENCE FOR FLOWERY PROSE
GILBERT, GILBERT
GILBERT WOULD NEVER COMPOSE
A SONNET TO MY EYES'

(**ANNE** *disappears.*)

DIANA. *(to the baby)* Your Auntie Anne sure mentions Gilbert a lot!

(reading again)

'ROY IS REGAL, HE'S ROYAL
IT'S HARD TO BELIEVE HE'S REAL
LIKE MY HERO HE'S LOYAL
HE'S AVERIL'S IDEAL'

Uh oh!

'HE'S NOT EXACTLY WORDSWORTH
BUT MY WORD
THE FELLOW TRIES

(**ANNE** *appears again.*)

DIANA & ANNE.

AND GILBERT WOULD NEVER COMPOSE
A SONNET TO MY EYES
GILBERT WOULD NEVER COMPOSE
HE HAS NO PATIENCE FOR FLOWERY PROSE
GILBERT, GILBERT. GILBERT WOULD NEVER COMPOSE
GILBERT IS NOT ONE OF THOSE
GILBERT WOULD NEVER COMPOSE
A SONNET TO MY EYES

(Lights dim on **DIANA & ANNE.***)*

(coming up immediately on)

(Marilla's kitchen.)

(**MARILLA** *is reading the news from Anne. She is gravely concerned.* **MRS. LYNDE** *snoops in.*)

MRS. LYNDE. Anything interesting come in the mail?

MARILLA. No!

MRS. LYNDE. Why, Marilla Cuthbert!

MARILLA. Go back to your own kitchen, Rachel!

MRS. LYNDE.

> YOU'VE A SECRET, I CAN SMELL IT
> IF YOU CARE FOR ME, YOU'LL TELL IT
> IS THAT A LETTER FROM ANNE YOU HOLD?
> IF SHE HAS NEWS I SHOULD BE TOLD
> I'M PRACTICALLY FAMILY

MARILLA. *(blurting it out bitterly)* It looks as if Anne will be getting engaged!

MRS. LYNDE.

> ANNE AND GILBERT
> I KNEW IT! I KNEW IT!
> I'VE ALWAYS SAID THAT THOSE TWO WOULD DO IT
> SUCH A HANDSOME PAIR, I CONFESS
> I PLANNED TO GIVE HER MY OWN WEDDING DRESS
> ANNE AND GILBERT. I SAW IT! I SAW IT!
> HER HEART WAS ICY
> BUT GILBERT COULD THAW IT

MARILLA. It isn't Gilbert, Rachel. It's a man from....

(The worst thing possible)

away!

Royal Gardner.

(Fighting tears as she spits out)

He's a millionaire!

MRS. LYNDE. Well!

> I'VE HAD A KIND OF SECOND SIGHT
> SINCE I WAS A YOUNG WEE LASS
> AND ALL THE THINGS THAT I'VE PREDICTED
> ALWAYS CAME TO PASS
> AND I'D SAY 'ANNE & GILBERT. MARK MY WORD WE'LL SEE
>   THEM WED'
> YOU'RE NEVER SAFE FROM SURPRISES TILL YOU'RE DEAD

REMEMBER THE TIME AWAY BACK WHEN
WE LAUGHED TO BEAT THE BAND
YOU SENT AWAY FOR AN ORPHAN BOY
TO BE THE HIRED HAND
YOU WANTED A BIG BRAW BURLY LAD
GOT A SLIP OF A GIRL INSTEAD
YOU'RE NEVER SAFE FROM SURPRISES TILL YOU'RE DEAD

MRS. LYNDE. *(cont.)*

YOU'RE NEVER SAFE, YOU NEVER KNOW
JUST WHICH WAY THE WIND WILL BLOW
THAT WRETCHED DAY I CAN'T FORGET
MY APPLE JELLY WOULDN'T SET
AND WHEN YOUR ANNE WAS JUST THIRTEEN
SHE GRABBED HER HAIR AND DYED IT GREEN
MY LIPS GOT THIN, MY WAIST GOT THICK
MY COUSIN MARRIED A CATHOLIC

MARILLA. Refresh my memory, Rachel, what did you do?

MRS. LYNDE. What could we do? We went into deep mourning for three years.

Then we graciously forgave her.

But I tell you, Marilla, I'm bowled over by this news about Anne!

WE'VE SEEN AND HEARD THE DARNDEST THINGS
SINCE WE GOT LONG IN THE TOOTH
WHY, REMEMBER THE TIME THE MINISTER LIED
AND THE PREMIER TOLD THE TRUTH?
AND NOW I HEAR OUR CLEVER ANNE
IS A REGULAR DUNDERHEAD!!
YOU'RE NEVER SAFE FROM SURPRISES TILL YOU'RE DEAD

(Lights dim on them.)

(At still another area of the stage, a spot picks up **JOSIE.***)*

JOSIE. *(with a huge smile)*

GILBERT, GILBERT, HAVE YOU HEARD?
THERE'S A MESSAGE HERE FOR YOU
ANNE HAS FOUND ANOTHER
YOU'LL BE LIKE HER BROTHER
YOU WILL NEED A SWEETHEART KIND AND TRUE

JOSIE. *(cont.)*

> WILL I EVER STAND A CHANCE?
> DON'T YOU EVER THINK OF ME?
> THOUGH YOU CAN'T HAVE ANNE
> CONSIDER IF YOU CAN
> THE OTHER GIRL IN AVONLEA
> SWEET LITTLE JOSIE
> THE OTHER GIRL IN AVONLEA
>
> *(Blackout)*

Scene Five

(A ladies' dressing room at Redmond.)

*(**PHIL** is at a dressing table. The rest of the **GIRLS** are peering out the window in a state of anticipation.)*

GIRLS.

EVERY YOUNG GIRL AT REDMOND U.
GOES TO PIECES AT THE THOUGHT OF A RENDEZVOUS
WITH A CERTAIN BOY
SHE COULD GAZE UPON FOR HOURS
GILBERT BLYTHE
WHO MAKES THE GIRLS OF REDMOND U. SIGH
GILBERT BLYTHE
THE MMMM-MMMM-MMMM BOY FROM P.E.I.
GILBERT BLYTHE
WHO'S COMING TO DELIVER
FLOWERS

*(**ANNE** enters in a beautiful gown. She heads straight for **PHIL**.)*

PHIL. Oh, Anne, you look like Cinderella.

ANNE. It's the dress. My favourite! Of yours!

PHIL. Well, I haven't worn two gowns to a ball YET!

GIRLS.

ONE OF THE WONDERS OF THIS PLACE
IS THAT EVERYWHERE YOU TURN
YOU SEE GILBERT'S FACE
PAINTING BUGGIES BLUE
EVEN CLEANING OUT THE LOO
GILBERT BLYTHE
WHO GIVES THE GIRLS AT REDMOND ONE DREAM
GILBERT BLYTHE
THE CAPTAIN OF THE FRESHMAN FOOTBALL TEAM
GILBERT BLYTHE
I THANK YOU FOR THE FLOWERS
GILBERT BLYTHE

ANNE. Oh my! Is Gil really considered THAT good looking?

PHIL. My goodness, yes! Most of Redmond thinks you were insane to reject him in Avonlea.

You're blushing, Queen Anne.

ANNE. I wonder how 'most of Redmond' found out what happened in Avonlea.

I don't recall telling anyone but you.

PHIL. Well, you can't stop the news.

But you've proven you're not insane.

Who could have foreseen that you were destined to hook Roy Gardner?

ANNE. I don't think I've 'hooked' Roy Gardner.

PHIL. Come on and tell me, Anne: you do love Roy, don't you?

ANNE. I…I suppose so.

PHIL. But you're not blushing.

GIRL AT WINDOW. HERE HE COMES!

(The GIRLS rush away from the window to the mirrors for last minute touch ups.)

PHIL. Of course Roy is awfully handsome.

Not to mention rich.

Richer than me and that's impressive!

But Gilbert.

What can you say about Gilbert?

Oh, Anne?

ANNE. Yes?

PHIL. NOW, you're blushing!

ANNE. I am?

PHIL. You am!

I hear he's got a perfectly gorgeous date for the reception.

(GILBERT enters in delivery overalls. He gives out boxes to the GIRLS.)

ANNE. *(whispering to PHIL)* I am glad Gilbert's got a…gorgeous date.

PHIL. Then why are you still blushing?

(**GILBERT** *approaches* **ANNE & PHIL.**)

GILBERT. Hi, Phil. Hello, Anne. You both look beautiful.

ANNE. And you look industrious. Aren't you going to the reception?

GILBERT. I planned my route so that this would be my last stop.

*(***GILBERT*** suddenly opens the overalls revealing a tux with tails. He looks great. The* **GIRLS** *are visibly moved. One momentarily faints. All this goes completely unnoticed by* **GILBERT.***)*

PHIL. I hear you have some glamorous mystery date visiting.

GILBERT. Well, she is rather glamorous but not much of a mystery.

Anne knows her well. It's Josie Pye!

ANNE. JOSIE PYE!!!

(forcing a smile)

Here?

GILBERT. I'm surprised she hasn't been writing you.

She's done well enough with her studies that she's thinking of applying to Redmond.

She wanted to see the place before she decided so I offered to be her guide.

I thought she might enjoy the reception tonight.

PHIL. *(with deliberate timing)* I'd better go ahead.

(looking at the two corsages)

I should make a decision too!

Alec or Alonzo?

(She ponders for a moment. Then throws both corsages to the **GIRLS**, *at least two of whom are thrilled. And off* **PHIL** *goes.)*

GILBERT. *(giving* **ANNE** *a box)* This one's yours. From Roy Gardner, I presume.

It's shockingly expensive!

But you won't like it.

ANNE. Won't I?

(opening the box, determined to love it)

I'm sure it's lovely. It's

(Of course, she hates it.)

…an orchid.

GILBERT. I didn't sell it to him, I only packed the order.

ANNE. Perfect with this dress!

GILBERT. Except you don't like orchids.

ANNE. I never said that!

GILBERT.

YOU ONCE TOLD ME
YOU COULD NEVER REALLY WARM UP TO A FLOWER
YOU COULDN'T LIVE WITH
YOU ONCE TOLD ME
I REMEMBER, WE DISCUSSED IT FOR AN HOUR
'WHAT YOU COULD LIVE WITH'
I PAID VERY CLOSE ATTENTION
AND I'LL MENTION IF I MAY
I HEARD YOU SAY THAT YOU WOULD NOT
EVER WEAR A HOT HOUSE FLOWER

And I quote;

'HOT HOUSE FLOWERS
AREN'T LIKE FLOWERS THAT HAVE FLOWERED IN A GARDEN
OR IN A FOREST
HOT HOUSE FLOWERS AREN'T FOR ME'
IF I MISQUOTE I BEG YOUR PARDON
I'M JUST THE FLORIST
'I'D FEEL SILLY
WHERE I COULDN'T WEAR A LILY TO A DANCE'

YOU WON'T BE HAPPY
WITH A FLOWER YOU CAN'T LIVE WITH
THAT'S NO WAY TO GO TO THE DANCE
DON'T GO WITH THE WRONG FLOWER
YOU WON'T BE HAPPY
YOU WON'T BE HAPPY
BUT WEAR THE RIGHT FLOWER TO THE DANCE
AND YOU'LL BE HAPPY AT THE DANCE

GIRLS.

>HOT HOUSE FLOWERS AREN'T LIKE FLOWERS
>THAT HAVE FLOWERED UP LIKE HEATHER
>HEATHER IS HEARTY
>HOT HOUSE FLOWERS DON'T GET OUT
>THEY'RE UNAFFECTED BY THE WEATHER
>GOOD FOR A PARTY

GILBERT.

>I KNOW FLOWERS
>AND YOU'RE RUNNING OUT OF HOURS TO THE DANCE

GILBERT & GIRLS.

>YOU WON'T BE HAPPY
>WITH A FLOWER YOU CAN'T LIVE WITH
>THAT'S NO WAY TO GO TO THE DANCE
>DON'T GO WITH THE WRONG FLOWER
>YOU WON'T BE HAPPY
>YOU WON'T BE HAPPY
>BUT WEAR THE RIGHT FLOWER TO THE DANCE
>AND YOU'LL BE HAPPY AT THE DANCE

>(**GILBERT** *pulls a lily and some ribbon out of a bag and goes to work making a corsage.*)

GIRLS.

>(*as* **GILBERT** *makes the corsage*)

>GILBERT BLYTHE
>GILBERT BLYTHE
>YOU LOOK SO BEAUTIFUL
>GILBERT BLYTHE
>GILBERT BLYTHE
>YOU'RE JUST SO WONDERFUL TO SEE
>GILBERT BLYTHE
>GILBERT BLYTHE
>MR. FLOWER MAN
>YOU CAN ALWAYS PIN LILIES ON ME

>(*The* **GIRLS** *repeat the above again while* **GILBERT** *sings.*)

GILBERT.

> YOU WON'T BE HAPPY
> WITH A FLOWER YOU CAN'T LIVE WITH
> THAT'S NO WAY TO GO TO THE DANCE
> DON'T GO WITH THE WRONG FLOWER
> YOU WON'T BE HAPPY

GIRLS.

> YOU WON'T BE HAPPY

GILBERT.

> YOU WON'T BE HAPPY

GIRLS.

> YOU WON'T BE HAPPY

GILBERT & GIRLS.

> BUT WEAR THE RIGHT FLOWER TO THE DANCE
> AND YOU'LL BE HAPPY AT THE DANCE

> *(He presents the newly completed corsage to* **ANNE***. Then he leaves. For a moment,* **ANNE** *sits there looking at her two corsages.)*

> *(The lights dim out, coming up immediately on the reception.)*

Scene Six

(The Reception)

(The dance is in full swing. **ANNE** *enters with* **ROY**. *She is wearing the lily. They begin to waltz.)*

ROY. Didn't you get my orchid?

ANNE. Yes, I did and it was lovely, but –

ROY. But it didn't suit your gown. In the future we'll have to confer in advance.

ANNE. You always seem to say the perfect thing.

ROY. And I can sing a popular tune of the day, too.

ANNE. Really?

ROY.

> I WENT MY LONELY WAY
> I FILLED EACH LONELY DAY
> JUST WHEN I'D GIVEN UP HOPE
>
> SOMEHOW YOU CAME ALONG
> MY LIFE BECAME A SONG
> JUST WHEN I'D GIVEN UP HOPE
>
> I NEVER THOUGHT THAT YOU AND I
> WOULD WIND UP IN A DANCE
> I NEVER THOUGHT I'D HAVE THE NERVE
> TO TAKE A CHANCE
>
> I'VE BEEN ALONE BEFORE
> I'LL BE ALONE NO MORE
> JUST WHEN I'D GIVEN UP HOPE

(Dance. **ANNE & ROY** *seem to be the centre of attention.* **JOSIE PYE** *sees them. She is thrilled.)*

JOSIE.

> ANNE IS IN LOVE I SEE
> GILBERT IS FINALLY FREE
> JUST WHEN I'D GIVEN UP HOPE
>
> THIS MIGHT JUST BE THE DAY
> GILBERT LOOKS JOSIE'S WAY
> JUST WHEN I'D GIVEN UP HOPE

(JOSIE stares at GILBERT at the other end of the dance floor, fetching punch. ROY gazes at ANNE.)

JOSIE & ROY.

I NEVER THOUGHT THAT YOU AND I
WOULD WIND UP IN A DANCE
I NEVER THOUGHT I'D HAVE THE NERVE
TO TAKE A CHANCE

JOSIE.

ANNE'S GOT HER 'SONNETEER'
GILBERT, I'M OVER HERE
JUST WHEN I'D GIVEN UP HOPE

(Dance. GILBERT, each hand holding a punch cup, tries to make his way across the floor to JOSIE. The DANCERS get in his way. After a moment, they part and for the first time, GILBERT sees that ANNE has his lily on.)

GILBERT.

SHE'S PINNED MY LILY ON
ANNE'S GOT MY LILY ON
JUST WHEN I'D GIVEN UP HOPE

(JOSIE takes note of GILBERT staring at ANNE.)

SHE SAID SHE'D NEVER FALL
SHE'S FALLEN AFTER ALL
JUST WHEN I'D GIVEN UP HOPE

GILBERT, JOSIE & ROY.

I NEVER THOUGHT THAT YOU AND I
WOULD WIND UP IN A DANCE
I NEVER THOUGHT I'D HAVE THE NERVE
TO TAKE THE CHANCE

GILBERT.

ONCE I WAS WOEBEGONE
ANNE'S GOT MY LILY ON
JUST WHEN I'D GIVEN UP HOPE

JOSIE.

THIS IS NOT A GIRL FROM AVONLEA
WILLING TO BE WHINING AT SIXTY THREE;
'THIS WAS MY BIG CHANCE'
WHAT BIG CHANCE?
WHAT ROMANCE?

JOSIE. *(cont.)*

> I'M NOT AVERIL
> I'LL HAVE MORE THAN ONE IDEAL
> I'M NOT ANNE
> DON'T HAVE A HEART THAT'S MADE OF STEEL
> WHAT KIND OF PYE
> AM I
> IF I CAN'T CUT BAIT?
> I'M NOT LIKE GILBERT
> I JUST CAN'T WAIT

ALL GUESTS.

> I WENT MY LONELY WAY
> I FILLED EACH LONELY DAY
> JUST WHEN I'D GIVEN UP HOPE
>
> SOMEHOW YOU CAME ALONG
> MY LIFE BECAME A SONG
> JUST WHEN I'D GIVEN UP HOPE

JOSIE.

> I'VE GIVEN UP HOPE

ALL GUESTS. (**ANNE & GILBERT** *sing behind them in a round.*)

> I NEVER THOUGHT THAT YOU AND I
> WOULD WIND UP IN A DANCE
> I NEVER THOUGHT I'D HAVE THE NERVE
> TO TAKE A CHANCE
>
> I'VE BEEN ALONE BEFORE
> I'LL BE ALONE NO MORE
> JUST WHEN I'D GIVEN UP HOPE
> JUST WHEN I'D GIVEN UP
> JUST WHEN I'D GIVEN UP
> JUST WHEN I'D GIVEN UP HOPE

ROY.

> JUST WHEN I'D GIVEN UP HOPE
>
> *(On the last note,* **ANNE** *looks at* **GILBERT**. *She quickly looks back at* **ROY**, *who is applauding the orchestra. She applauds too.)*

JOSIE. You really are still in love with Anne, aren't you Gilbert?

(Music begins.)

GILBERT. I never said that I wasn't!

JOSIE. But Gilbert, LOOK at her!

GILBERT. I'm looking! And she's wearing my lily!

JOSIE. That means something?

GILBERT. She may not know it but I think it does.

JOSIE. Gilbert, you are an idiot.

GILBERT. I know.

But I love her, Josie.

JOSIE. Alright, Gilbert! I'm going to help you.

GILBERT. And why would you do that?

JOSIE. I get the feeling I owe it to posterity.

And the only reason I can use posterity in a sentence is because of relentless old Anne.

What finer thank you gift could I give her...than you?

Get her to dance with you.

GILBERT. I was planning THAT!

JOSIE. But to an Island tune.

Something she knows from home.

You know how Anne is about home.

You gotta get her where she's vulnerable.

GILBERT. An Island tune? It's not likely to happen with this orchestra!

JOSIE. Where's Moody?

GILBERT. Right over there but he's given up the fiddle!

JOSIE. You find a fiddle! Leave Moody to me!

(GILBERT goes off as JOSIE rushes over to MOODY.)

Say, Moody –

MOODY. JOSIE PYE!

JOSIE. How'd you like to dance every dance for the rest of the evening with me?

MOODY. That wouldn't be bad.

What do I have to do?

And remember I'm going to be a minister.

JOSIE. Me too!

All you have to do is play one little Island fiddle tune.

MOODY. But I left my fiddle on the Island.

(GILBERT joins them.)

GILBERT. *(producing a fiddle)* I just borrowed this from the orchestra for twenty-five cents.

(MOODY starts the fiddle tune. JOSIE leads GILBERT onto the dance floor.)

GILBERT.

IF YOU'RE PLEASED AS PUNCH WITH WHERE YOU LIVE
AND PROUD OF WHAT YOU DO
YOU'RE ISLAND
YOU'RE ISLAND THROUGH AND THROUGH

AND IF YOU MIND YOUR BUSINESS
AND YOU MIND YOUR NEIGHBOUR'S TOO
YOU'RE ISLAND, YOU'RE ISLAND THROUGH AND THROUGH

JOSIE.

IF PARLOURS ARE FOR VISITORS
AND FRIDAYS ARE FOR FISH
IF THERE HAS TO BE A BOILED SPUD
ON EACH AND EVERY DISH

GILBERT & JOSIE.

IF A LITTLE SMUDGE OF RED MUD'S
THE POLISH ON YOUR SHOE
YOU'RE ISLAND, YOU'RE ISLAND THROUGH AND THROUGH

GILBERT. *(at ANNE)*

IF YOU HAVE MORE FRECKLES ON YOUR FACE
THEN TURNIPS IN A STEW
YOU'RE ISLAND, YOU'RE ISLAND THROUGH AND THROUGH

JOSIE.

IF YOU DROP IN UNEXPECTEDLY

JOSIE & GILBERT.

JUST WHEN THE TEA IS DUE
YOU'RE ISLAND, YOU'RE ISLAND THROUGH AND THROUGH

MOODY.

> IF YOU THINK THAT EATING SPICY FOOD
> IS JUST A SIGN OF GREED

ANNE. *(jumping in)*

> AND PORRIDGE AND POTATOES
> ARE ALL YOU REALLY NEED

ALL FOUR.

> IF THE JIGS AND REELS CAN HIT YOU
> LIKE A WALTZ WOULD NEVER DO
> YOU'RE ISLAND, YOU'RE ISLAND THROUGH AND THROUGH

> *(ANNE heads back to ROY.)*

> YOU'RE ISLAND YOU'RE ISLAND
> YOU'RE FROM PRINCE EDWARD ISLAND
> YOU'RE ISLAND, YOU'RE ISLAND THROUGH AND THROUGH

> YOU'RE ISLAND YOU'RE ISLAND
> YOU'RE FROM PRINCE EDWARD ISLAND
> YOU'RE ISLAND, YOU'RE ISLAND THROUGH AND THROUGH

> *(As **MOODY** launches into the dance, **ANNE** quickly finds herself drawn into it, dancing next to and eventually with **GILBERT**. Then)*

ALL FOUR.

> IF SUNDAY FINDS YOU WITH YOUR FAMILY
> YAWNING IN THE PEW
> YOU'RE ISLAND, YOU'RE ISLAND THROUGH AND THROUGH

> IF YOU BELIEVE THAT YOUR FARM
> IT HAS THE FINEST VIEW
> YOU'RE ISLAND, YOU'RE ISLAND THROUGH AND THROUGH

GILBERT. *(right at ROY)*

> AND IF YOU THINK THE MAN WHO THINKS HE'S SPECIAL
> IS A FOOL

ROY. *(challenged)*

> AND SOMEONE TOO AMBITIOUS
> WILL TASTE YOUR RIDICULE

ANNE. *(coming between them)*

> IF YOU DON'T BELIEVE IN GIVING PRAISE
> TILL PRAISE IS OVERDUE
> YOU'RE ISLAND, YOU'RE ISLAND THOUGH AND THROUGH

ALL.

> YOU'RE ISLAND YOU'RE ISLAND
> YOU'RE FROM PRINCE EDWARD ISLAND
> YOU'RE ISLAND, YOU'RE ISLAND THROUGH AND THROUGH
>
> YOU'RE ISLAND YOU'RE ISLAND
> YOU'RE FROM PRINCE EDWARD

> *(As* **MOODY** *hams it up a bit on his fiddle,* **PHIL** *takes her first good look at him. She is fascinated.* **MOODY** *notices her staring. They are both in love at first sight. All focus is on them as* **PHIL** *walks to* **MOODY** *as though in a trance as he plays a cadenza. There is a moment of sublime silence as they stare into each others eyes. But then* **MOODY** *gets back to the business of the dance.)*

ALL.

> YOU'RE ISLAND YOU'RE ISLAND
> YOU'RE FROM PRINCE EDWARD ISLAND
> YOU'RE ISLAND, YOU'RE ISLAND THROUGH AND THROUGH
> YOU'RE ISLAND
> YOU'RE ISLAND
> YOU'RE ISLAND
> YOU'RE ISLAND
> YOU'RE ISLAND THROUGH AND THROUGH

> *(On the last note of the song,* **ANNE,** *flushed and blushing looking at* **GILBERT,** *suddenly turns, rushes to* **ROY** *and kisses him.* **ANNE** *and* **ROY** *go off,* **ANNE** *not even daring to look at* **GILBERT.** **JOSIE** *goes to him, but he hurries off.)*

> *(Lights dim out.)*

Scene Seven

(Outside the dance.)

*(Lights suddenly come up on **PHIL**.)*

PHIL.

I ALWAYS THOUGHT THE MAN FOR ME
WOULD BE A MAN WITH MONEY
AND HE WOULD SPEND A PILE ON ME
BEFORE I'D CALL HIM HONEY
A MAN OF MEANS WITH LOTS OF BEANS
AND GOOD OLD MONEYED CHARM
BUT THAT WAS BEFORE I MET THE BOY
WITH THE PERMANENT CROOK IN HIS ARM

THAT LITTLE FIDDLE PLAYER
THAT LITTLE FIDDLE PLAYER
HE'S THE ONE I'LL MARRY
THAT LITTLE FIDDLE PLAYER
THAT LITTLE FIDDLE PLAYER
IT'S QUITE NECESSARY
HE DOESN'T KNOW, BUT I KNEW
THE MOMENT I HEARD HIM PLAY
THAT LITTLE FIDDLE PLAYER STOLE MY HEART AWAY

HE'S NOT THE HANDSOMEST OF MEN
THAT CANNOT BE DENIED
BUT SUDDENLY I CARE ABOUT
THE THINGS THAT ARE INSIDE
HE WON'T BE RICH AND THAT'S A SWITCH
BUT I WILL TAKE A CHANCE
I'M TINGLING IMAGINING
SATURDAY NIGHT AT THE MANSE

One, two, three, enter the Boys!

*(**ALEC & ALONZO** rush on.)*

THAT LITTLE FIDDLE PLAYER
THAT LITTLE FIDDLE PLAYER
WAS CREATED FOR ME
THAT LITTLE FIDDLE PLAYER

THAT LITTLE FIDDLE PLAYER
HE WILL NEVER BORE ME
I'LL FEEL LIKE I'M IN HEAVEN
WHEN MOODY SAYS "LET US PRAY"

PHIL. *(cont.)* Okay!

THAT LITTLE FIDDLE PLAYER STOLE MY HEART AWAY

WHO WOULD HAVE THOUGHT IT?
KNOWING MY HISTORY WITH BEAUX
THEY ALL ADORED ME
THEY HAD THEIR REASONS HEAVEN KNOWS
BUT WHO'D HAVE GUESSED IT?
WHAT A SURPRISE FOR EVERYONE
I'VE FOUND A MAN OF SUBSTANCE
WHO KNOWS HOW TO HAVE FUN

THAT LITTLE FIDDLE PLAYER

ALEC & ALONZO.

THAT LITTLE FIDDLE PLAYER?

PHIL.

GONNA BE IN CLOVER
THAT LITTLE FIDDLE PLAYER

ALEC & ALONZO.

THAT LITTLE FIDDLE PLAYER?

PHIL.

WHEN I WIN HIM OVER

ALL THREE.

CAN YOU IMAGINE PHIL
AS THE MINISTER'S FIANCEE?

PHIL.

THAT LITTLE FIDDLE PLAYER

ALEC & ALONZO.

THAT LITTLE FIDDLE PLAYER

PHIL.

THAT LITTLE FIDDLE PLAYER

ALEC.

THAT LITTLE

ALONZO.

THAT LITTLE

PHIL.

THAT LITTLE FIDDLE PLAYER

ALEC & ALONZO.

THAT LITTLE THAT THAT THAT LITTLE FIDDLE PLAYER

PHIL.

THAT LITTLE FIDDLE PLAYER

ALEC & ALONZO.

THAT LITTLE FIDDLE PLAYER

PHIL.

THAT LITTLE

ALEC & ALONZO.

THAT LITTLE

ALL THREE.

THAT LITTLE LITTLE THAT

ALEC & ALONZO.

THAT LITTLE

PHIL.

FIDDLE PLAYER
THAT LITTLE FIDDLE PLAYER
STOLE MY HEART AWAY

(MOODY enters and shows off a little with his fiddle.)

ALL THREE.

AMEN

(PHIL takes MOODY's arm and goes off with him leaving a stunned ALEC & ALONZO behind. JOSIE walks by with her suitcase. The "Here Come Those Beaux Again" theme plays. ALEC & ALONZO see JOSIE and smile. They follow her off, much as they did PHIL.)

(Blackout)

(Lights come up immediately on Charlotte's Café.)

Scene Eight

(Charlotte's Café)

(ANNE enters with a suitcase.)

HEAD WAITER. *(A not very happy man.)* Welcome to Charlotte's Cafe.

ANNE. Mr. Gardner's table, please.

HEAD WAITER. Mr. Gardner! Of course! May I take your bag? MR. BLYTHE!

(GILBERT joins them.)

Please escort this lovely lady to Mr. Gardner's table.

GILBERT. *(imitating the head waiter's formal tone)* This way, Madam!

ANNE. You work here, too?

GILBERT. I haven't sold any stories to *CANADIAN WOMAN* lately.

(ANNE lets that one slide. GILBERT smiles.)

On your way home for the summer?

ANNE. I miss Avonlea so. When are you coming?

GILBERT. Not this year!

The price of the rail ticket and the extra hours I can get around here when everyone else has gone home go straight into the medical school kitty.

Anne! I just happen to have your birthday present in my locker.

I was going to send it along with Moody.

ANNE. Gilbert, I can't accept a present from you.

GILBERT. Why not?

Is it because congratulations are in order?

ANNE. No! Not yet.

GILBERT. No?

(PHIL has entered the Café and joins them.)

PHIL. Hello, all! My, what have I walked in on?

(The **HEAD WAITER** *hisses at* **GILBERT**.*)*

GILBERT. Excuse me.

(He rushes off.)

PHIL. You're blushing!

*(**ANNE** tries to turn away from her.)*

ANNE. I'm here to meet Roy! He's seeing me off on the train.

PHIL. Now, Queen Anne, don't fuss! I've turned over a new leaf.

ANNE. You?

*(**MOODY** comes over to seat them, not knowing who they are.)*

MOODY. May I take your order? PHILIPPA?

(an afterthought)

Hello, Anne.

PHIL. I just happened to run into Anne. I'm really here for another good look at you!

(She grabs and kisses him. The stunned **HEAD WAITER** *rushes to stop this display.)*

HEAD WAITER. WHAT is going on around here? MCPHERSON, YOU'RE FIRED!

*(He sees **PHIL**.)*

Philippa Gordon! MCPHERSON, JUST KIDDING!

(He rushes back to his post.)

PHIL. Just bring us some tea, honey. I'll wait with Anne till Roy gets here or you have a break; whichever comes first!

*(**MOODY** goes off, a very happy man.)*

PHIL. *(to* **ANNE**) As impressive a prospect as Royal Gardner may be, I've never quite understood how you could prefer him to let's say...Gilbert!

PHIL. *(cont.)* There's that blush again.

But I choose to ignore that blush!

Because I myself would prefer Moody to Gilbert.

As strange as THAT may seem!

I never thought I could fall in love with such a homely man!

Not to mention: poor!

There! I said it! He's poor!

He works here as a waiter and I think it's cute!

ANNE. You really are serious!

PHIL. I'll be following you to Avonlea to meet his family.

He doesn't know it yet, poor dear!

But I'm sure, Anne.

This is what I want. I'm going to be a minister's wife in Avonlea!

ANNE. The signs are that Roy is about to propose.

PHIL. And you're about to accept?

(ROY enters.)

ROY. Hello, Miss Gordon. Are you joining us?

PHIL. No, Mr. Gardner. I'm meeting my intended, Mr. McPherson.

ROY. MOODY SPURGEON MACPHERSON?

PHIL. Spurgeon?

ANNE. Spurgeon!

PHIL. Even that doesn't bother me.

I really must love him!

(She heads to another table. ROY sits down.)

ROY. We've been avoiding any mention of a couple of subjects.

ANNE. Then it's up to you to weave them into the conversation!

(GILBERT goes up to PHIL)

GILBERT. Phil, is Anne going to marry that guy?

PHIL. Ask me in five!

ROY. The first subject is matrimony.

(ANNE's *carefree attitude disappears.* GILBERT *watches her with* PHIL. MOODY *joins them.*)

GILBERT. I know that look!

MOODY. Me too!

(GILBERT & PHIL *look at* MOODY.)

ANNE. I can't marry you, Roy!

ROY. *(stunned)* What do you mean?

ANNE. I thought I could, but I can't.

ROY. WHY can't you?

ANNE. *(realizing it this moment)* Because I don't care enough for you.

ROY. *(dramatically, a little bit of the spoiled boy, throwing a fit)* So, you've just been amusing yourself all these months? Well, I hope you were suitably amused.

Because you have RUINED my life!

(*He stalks out of the cafe.* GILBERT & MOODY *turn away.* PHIL *goes to* ANNE.)

PHIL. Anne?

ANNE. I led him on shamelessly!

PHIL. Now, I'm not the kind of girl to say 'I told you so.' Oh, yes I am!

ANNE. I couldn't marry Roy.

PHIL. Because?

ANNE. It's NOT because of Gilbert! Is he still staring?

PHIL. What do you think?

ANNE. I've led him on too! I'm still leading him on!

I just don't know what I want!

(*She thinks.*)

Isn't this ridiculous?

I want my mother!.

GILBERT. Did she just say she wants her mother?

MOODY. Something like that!

GILBERT. I've got what she needs!

MOODY. That's a matter of opinion, Gil!

GILBERT. No! In my locker, I've got what she needs!

MOODY. Her mother?

HEAD WAITER. Blythe, I've never had a problem with you before!

Take care of your tables now or you're fired!

Mr. McPherson, you're doing great!

GILBERT. Then I quit!

It's not the first job I've quit for Anne!

And I think I just might be going home for the summer after all.

I'll go clean out my locker.

PHIL. Maybe you should go see, what's her name, Marulla!

ANNE. Marilla!

PHIL. Exactly.

ANNE. Marilla's already given me her advice, about Gilbert. Marilla is alone.

And it's she who raised me.

I'm just like her. Stubborn.

(**GILBERT** *gets to the table with a small parcel and sits down at the table.*)

GILBERT. You? 'Stubborn?' Anne, where would you get an idea like that?

ANNE. Gilbert, this is NOT the right time for you to –

GILBERT. Oh, I think it is!

PHIL. And I think it's time for me to set sail.

Dad's going to disinherit me when I marry Moody.

I'd better shop while the shopping's good!

(*She rushes off.*)

ANNE. Gil, please –

GILBERT. Seriously, Anne, aren't we still friends?

ANNE. Of course we are, but –

GILBERT. Then let me give you your birthday present!

ANNE. It isn't my birthday yet!

GILBERT. I had to make a courier trip to Bolingbroke, last week.

I had some free time before my train back and I did a little detective work.

The house you were born in, 235 Belvedere Lane, has been torn down.

ANNE. You went looking for the house I was born in?

GILBERT. I thought it might please you.

The lot was owned by an old man across the street.

He remembered the Shirleys.

ANNE. He remembered my parents?

GILBERT. He even remembered you. He said you were the loudest baby he'd ever heard.

I told him you haven't changed much.

He still had these letters left behind after your mum and dad passed on.

One is from your dad to your mum.

One is from your mum to your dad.

And the last is from your dad....to you.

(She takes the letters from him. Music begins)

ANNE. *(stunned)* Gilbert, I haven't a single thing that belonged to my parents!

I don't know what to say!

GILBERT. That's a first!

Happy birthday, Anne.

(GILBERT goes off. ANNE looks at the letters.)

(Lights dim to a spot on ANNE.)

(The Café disappears as ANNE walks downstage looking at the first of the letters.)

ANNE. 'To Miss Bertha Willis! Her maiden name was Willis! Well!

*(**ANNE** sits down on the edge of the stage as she opens the first letter.)*

'My dear Miss Willis,' They must have just met!

'My dear Miss Willis,

HARD TO EXPLAIN WHO I WAS
BEFORE I WAS WITH YOU
I THOUGHT THAT I WAS ALONE
AND YOU THOUGHT YOU WERE TOO
I HAD MY FRIENDS
I HAD MY LIFE
I NEVER THOUGHT I'D HAVE A WIFE
BUT THEN WE MET
AND THEN WE DANCED
AND THEN I KNEW
THAT LOVE IS POSSIBLE
I NEVER THOUGHT THAT THAT COULD BE
OH HOW I HOPE YOUR HOME WILL BE WITH ME'

*(**ANNE** now picks up a letter from her mother. She begins reading in a girlish, almost overly romantic sort of way.)*

'Walter, darling, I hope I'm not being too foolish, writing you a letter when you sleep so beautifully not three inches away from me.

Perhaps I'll get to say these things to you a hundred thousand more times.

*(**ANNE** is devastated to realize that this letter is a good-bye.)*

But I feel my strength slipping further and further away.

I truly don't expect to see the sunrise again.

You're so ill yourself. I haven't the heart to wake you.

Especially since there's truly nothing to be done.

NOT FOR A MOMENT HAVE I
HAD EVEN ONE REGRET
MINE'S A RELUCTANT GOODBYE
BUT DARLING DON'T FORGET
WE HAVE A CHILD

YOU MUST GO ON
AND KEEP HER SAFE WHEN I AM GONE
DO THAT FOR HER
DO THAT FOR ME
MAKE SURE SHE KNOWS
THAT LOVE IS POSSIBLE
THAT I WAS PROUD TO BE YOUR WIFE
FOR YOU BELONGED FOREVER IN MY LIFE'

(**ANNE** *puts the letter down. She is filled with joy*)

ANNE. *(cont.)*

FOREVER IN HER LIFE
SHE LOVED HIM
SHE WAS NOT AFRAID
HER LOVE WAS REAL
HER LOVE WAS NOT A CHORE

FOREVER IN MY LIFE
I'LL TREASURE THESE LETTERS
LETTERS OF THEIR LOVE
A KIND OF LOVE
I'VE NEVER KNOWN BEFORE
AND I AM NOT AN ORPHAN ANYMORE

(She picks up the final letter.)

'To Anne from Dad.

Dear Anne,

HARD TO EXPLAIN WHO WE WERE
WITH YOU HERE ON MY KNEE
YOU'RE GOING TO BLOSSOM AND GROW
WE WANTED SO TO SEE
THAT'S NOT TO BE
GOD CHANGED HIS MIND
IT'S ONLY LOVE WE LEAVE BEHIND
ANNE LISTEN WELL
A HEART IS EARNED
I HAVE LEARNED THAT LOVE IS POSSIBLE
I LOVE MY DAUGHTER AND MY WIFE
I HOPE MY LOVE IS STRONGER THAN MY LIFE'

(She puts the letter down.)

ANNE. *(cont.)*

FOREVER IN MY LIFE
I'M DIFFERENT
I'M THE DAUGHTER OF
A KIND OF LOVE
THAT NEVER GOES ASTRAY
FOREVER IN MY LIFE
I'LL TREASURE THESE LETTERS
LETTERS FROM THE PAST
OF LASTING LOVE
ENOUGH TO FILL EACH DAY
SO IT'S IN ME TO LOVE A MAN THAT WAY

(She suddenly and slowly realizes the truth; smiling, almost laughing at its inevitability.)

GILBERT LOVES ANNE OF GREEN GABLES
AND THOUGH SHE WON'T ADMIT IT'S TRUE
ANNE OF GREEN GABLES LOVES GILBERT TOO

(Lights come up on Avonlea.)

Scene Nine

(Avonlea. In front of the schoolhouse.)

(All of Avonlea has turned out for something. **DIANA** *and* **FRED** *with the baby,* **MARILLA** *and* **MRS. LYNDE**, *even* **PHIL** *and* **MOODY**.*)*

ALL.

GILBERT LOVES ANNE OF GREEN GABLES
AND ALL OF US HAVE ALWAYS KNOWN
ANNE OF GREEN GABLES
IS GILBERT'S OWN

GILBERT LOVES ANNE OF GREEN GABLES
AND THOUGH SHE WAS THE LAST TO KNOW
ANNE OF GREEN GABLES LOVES GILBERT SO

*(***GILBERT*** enters.* **ANNE** *sees him. Everyone stares. After a moment,* **ANNE** *bravely marches up to* **GILBERT**. *When she reaches him, she suddenly sinks to her knees in a gesture of proposal, offering the gold piece.)*

ALL.

GILBERT LOVES ANNE OF GREEN GABLES
GILBERT LOVES ANNE OF GREEN GABLES
AND ANNE OF GREEN GABLES LOVES GILBERT SO

(During the above, **GILBERT** *brings* **ANNE** *up and she jumps into his arms for a kiss.)*

(The curtain falls.)

PROPS LIST

ACT I

Scene 1: Schoolhouse, exterior and interior
3 chairs (school board meeting, interior)
Bench (exterior)
Skipping rope (chorus)
Book - novel (chorus)
Laundry basket with laundry and pins (chorus)
Laundry line (chorus)
Bath towel (chorus)
Bucket (chorus)
Book (chorus)
Rejection letter (Anne)
Manuscript (Anne)
Gold coin (Gilbert)

Other props, if needed:
Bucket of potatoes and scrub brush
Needlepoint

Scene 2: Green Gables kitchen
Kitchen table
Cutting board
Dishcloth
Chair
Lunch pail (Anne)
Sandwich on cheesecloth (Anne)
Apple (Anne)
Satchel w/journal, notebook, 2 textbooks & pencil (Anne)

Scene 3: Inside the schoolhouse

Scene 5: Small beach cove
Bath towel (Gilbert)
Canvas bag with 4 books, notepad, pencil (Gilbert)

Scene 6: The graveyard
7 tombstones
Flower (Anne)
Satchel bag (Anne – repeat)
Canvas bag (Gilbert – repeat)

Scene 7: Green Gables / Schoolhouse
Handkerchief (Anne)
Tea towel (Marilla)
12 student notebooks (chorus)
Josie Pye notebook (Josie)
16 hardcover books (Anne's desk)

Slingshot (Anthony Pye)
Rat/snake (Anthony Pye)
Whoopin' stick/pointer (Anne)

Scene 8: Train Station
Train/garden bench (with back)
Travelling bag (Lynde)

Scene 9: Outside the Schoolhouse
Stack of 3 books – attached (chorus)
Hockey skates (Paul)
Letter from Rollings Reliable Baking Powder (Diana)

Scene 11: Outside the Wedding
Crutch (Paul)
Bride's bouquet (Diana)
Bridesmaid's bouquet (Anne)
Diana's wedding ring (Gilbert/Diana)

ACT II

Scene 1: Redmond
9 Redmond Anthems
6 Letters from home (chorus)
Letter from Marilla to Anne (Anne)
Books (chorus – repeat)

Scene 2: Old St. John's Cemetery
7 Tombstones (repeat)
Garden bench (repeat)
Letter (Anne – repeat)

Scene 3: Cemetery (cont'd)
Umbrella (Roy)

Scene 4: Avonlea / Redmond / Green Gables Kitchen
Chair and footstool (Diana)
Letter from Anne to Diana (Diana)
Letter from Anne to Marilla (Marilla)
Darning with attached needle (Marilla)
Eyeglasses & case (Marilla)
Letter & pencil, from Josie to Gilbert (Josie)

Scene 5: Dressing Room at Redmond
Large pouffe
3 café chairs
2 tables w/tablecloths
2 hand-held mirrors (girls/sophomores)
3 pairs of earrings (girls/sophomores)
3 pairs of long evening gloves (girls/sophomores)
3 pearl bracelets (girls/sophomores)

6 corsages in boxes (Anne (orchid), Phil (x2), girls/sophomores)
Lily for corsage (Gilbert/Anne)
Piece of lace (for Gilbert's lily corsage)

Scene 8: Charlotte's Café

2 café tables (repeat)
2 tablecloths
4 café chairs (3 repeat – from dressing room)
2 waiter towels & aprons (Gilbert, Moody)
Pencil & notepad (Moody)
Tea tray & service (Moody)
3 letters (Gilbert/Anne)

> 1) from Anne's father to her mother
> 2) from Anne's mother to her father
> 3) from Anne's father to Anne

Diana's baby (finale)

COSTUME PLOT

ANNE SHIRLEY

Avonlea
> Black tights
> Black shoes
> Plain cream blouse
> Cotton petticoat
> Green skirt w/ suspenders
> Green jacket
> Wig (red)

Green Gables Kitchen
> Plain blouse w/ brown ribbon
> Brown skirt
> Brown vest
> Brown jacket
> Straw hat, brown ribbon

Schoolhouse Interior
> Same – remove hat

Graveyard
> Underdress brown skirt
> Overdress cream pleated blouse
> Beige silk skirt w/ flounce
> Hat
> Black shoes
> Shawl

Avonlea
> Remove flounced skirt
> Remove shawl
> Add brown vest
> Add jacket onstage

Schoolhouse
> Cream blouse
> Brown cord. skirt
> Brown cord. vest
> Black boots

Wedding
> Crinoline
> Orange tiered bridesmaid dress
> Short lace gloves
> Beige shoes
> Remove fall from wig
> Long peach velvet cape

ACT 2

Redmond Campus
Cream+ blue dicky & bow
Blue skirt and jacket
Blue bag
Hat with blue band
Gloves

Dressing Room
Crinoline
Beige silk ball gown
Light tights
Beige shoes
Long white gloves
Hair ornament
Pearl necklace
remove fall from wig

Reception
Same

Café
Cream pleated blouse
Rough silk skirt w/ buttons
Hat
Suitcase
Replace fall in wig

Avonlea – Finale
Same

GILBERT BLYTHE

Avonlea
Underdressed: bathing suit
White shirt w/ Eton collar
Brown shoes / black socks
Light brown vest
Brown wool pants
Norfolk jacket
Brown paisley tie
Cap

Beach – Gilbert goes swimming
Remove (onstage) vest, shirt, pants, socks, shoes and jacket

Graveyard
Same as Avonlea
Rolled shirt sleeves
(Jacket off)

Wedding – Best Man
Wing collar shirt with cuff links

Grey/black striped pants
Grey vest
Black cravat
Black cutaway frock coat
Boutonniere
Black shoes

Redmond Campus

Beige shirt with Eton collar
Grey striped jacket
Grey vest
Grey pants
Black shoes
Grey tie

Dressing Room – the Flower Man
Underdress

White wing collar shirt
White pique bow tie & vest
Black tux pants
Black tail coat with tuck tails up
Pocket hanky
Lily preset in pocket
Black shoes and socks

Overdress

Navy blue shop coat
Cream cap

Reception

Remove shop coat and cap & release tails of tail coat
White gloves

Café

Beige cotton shirt
Black waiter vest
White waiter apron
Grey pants
Pewter arm bands
Black bow tie

Avonlea Finale – Gilbert

as in Act 1

MARILLA CUTHBERT
Avonlea-Carried Away

Plain blouse w/embroidery
Ochre skirt and cape
Green hat
Brown gloves
Bum pad & petticoat

Green Gables Kitchen
Pale green skirt
Print blouse
Apron
Black shoes
Mop cap

Avonlea
Same – remove apron & cap

Schoolhouse
As above – w/ apron

Train Station
Dark petticoat
Black blouse
Brown hat
Brown cape & skirt
Black gloves
Black bag

Schoolhouse
Same

Wedding
Ochre outfit/green hat
Light petticoat

ACT 2
Avonlea
Pale green cotton skirt
Print blouse as Act 1
Apron
Black shoes
Mop cap

Avonlea Finale
Beige blouse
Taupe/beige linen skirt
Black shoes

(Shawl for "My Beau" sequence and Finale)

RACHEL LYNDE
Schoolhouse
Bum pad
Cream petticoat
Black "socks" and shoes
Beige cotton blouse
Plum skirt with black trim
Plum cape with black trim
Plum hat
Handbag, gloves

Green Gables Kitchen & Schoolhouse
Same

Train Station
Black petticoat & bum pad
Black skirt and blouse
Black cape
Black mourning hat
Black gloves and shoes
Black handbag

Wedding
Same beige blouse
Plum skirt
Plum hat
Plum cape
Gloves and bag
Black shoes

ACT 2
Avonlea
Cream petticoat
Blue print skirt
Blue print blouse
Beige apron
Black shoes

Avonlea Finale
Beige flounced cotton skirt
Beige cotton blouse
Beige gloves
Beige hat
Black shoes

JOSIE PYE / FRESHETTE
Avonlea
Short petticoat
Bloomers
Two-tone grey dress, lace trim
Hair bow in wig
Dark tights and shoes

Beach
Blue sailor dress
Blue bloomers
Blue bow in hair – clip on
Straw hat
Knee high stockings *
Blue cotton shoes *
(*Remove onstage)

Schoolhouse
  Same as top of show

Wedding
  As in top of show
  Add grey/cream shawl

ACT 2
Redmond Campus (as Freshette)
  Striped green skirt
  Cream blouse
  Light tights
  Light shoes

Josie letter scene
  Long dress

Reception (as Josie)
  White crinoline
  Rose shot ball gown
  White tights
  Long gloves
  Hair ornament

DIANA BARRY / SOPHOMORE
Avonlea-Carried Away
  Light petticoat
  Light tights
  Beige shoes
  Lacy blouse
  Lilac scalloped skirt
  Wig (black)

Schoolhouse
  Add jacket and hat

Skating scene
  Rust skirt
  Mohair cape
  Cream blouse

Wedding (quick change)
  Crinoline
  White tights
  Beige shoes
  Wedding dress
  Quilted cape (put on onstage)
  Bridal veil
  Short white gloves

ACT 2
Redmond Campus (as sophomore)
  Cream blouse

Tan skirt
Red sweater
Glasses
Light tights and shoes

Avonlea (as Diana, pregnant)
Maternity padding
Plain blouse
Velvet suit w/red trim
Black tights and shoes

Dressing Room (as Dorm Girl)
Crinoline – cream tights
Blue velvet ball gown
Long satin gloves
Hair ornament
Rhinestone bracelet and earrings
Light tights and shoes

Avonlea Finale (as Diana)
Remove padding
Plain blouse
Maternity suit
Black boots and tights

PHILIPPA GORDON / MRS. PYE
Avonlea (as Mrs. Pye)
Long petticoat
Bum pad
Striped silk blouse
Bouclé skirt
Black tights and shoes

Wedding
As above
Add short cape with silk trim
Gloves and hat

ACT 2
Redmond Campus (as Philippa)
Textured cream outfit
Hat
Light tights and shoes
Bum pad under petticoat

Dressing Room
Crinoline
Cream tights
Red ball gown
Long cream gloves
Hair ornament
Rhinestone bracelet and earrings
Light tights and shoes

Café
> Red tapestry jacket and rust skirt
> Cream sleeveless blouse
> Long petticoat
> Dark tights
> Dark shoes

Avonlea Finale
> Same as Café scene

MOODY MACPHERSON

Avonlea-Carried Away
> Checked collarless shirt, rolled sleeves
> Beige overalls
> Brown cap
> Red or blue neckerchief
> Brown shoes

Wedding
> Beige shirt with stripe
> Brown tie
> Black socks and shoes
> Brown tie
> Brown pants

ACT 2

Redmond Campus
> Shirt with collar
> Plaid pants
> Beige sweater vest
> Brown tie

Reception
> White shirt
> Black two-piece suit
> Grey vest
> Grey tie
> White gloves
> Black shoes

Café
> Black pants / suspenders
> White shirt
> Black vest with velcro
> Black bow tie
> White waiter's apron
> Black shoes and socks
> Pewter armbands

Avonlea Finale – as wedding

ANTHONY PYE / ALEC

Avonlea (as Anthony Pye)
    Tights or knee socks
    Brown pants
    Dark checked shirt w/o collar
    Black shoes
    Wool cap

Wedding
    Beige shirt – Eton collar
    Beige sweater vest
    Bow tie

ACT 2

Redmond Campus (as Alec)
    Beige shirt with Eton collar
    Red sweater
    Brown pants
    Red sweater
    Bow tie (oversize)
    Black shoes

Reception (as Alec)
    Formal shirt with wing collar
    White vest w/ bow tie
    Black tux pants w/suspenders
    Black tail coat
    Black socks and shoes
    White gloves

Avonlea Finale (as Anthony Pye)
    Same as Act 1 wedding
    With bow tie
    Cap
    Beige sweater vest

MR. SLOANE/REVEREND/PROFESSOR/HEAD WAITER

Schoolhouse (as Mr. Sloane)
    Striped shirt w/ Eton collar
    Cuff links for shirt
    Green three-piece suit & tie
    Black bowler hat
    Glasses
    Gold watch and chain in vest
    Black shoes and socks

Avonlea "Island"
    Same as above – change to red knit vest
    No shirt
    Black pants with suspenders
    Navy uniform jacket

Navy visor cap
Gold watch / chain
Black shoes

Wedding (as Reverend)
Black shirt
Black pants
Clerical bib
Black robe

ACT 2
Redmond Campus (as Professor)
Striped shirt
Black pants
Red vest
Red bow tie
Black graduation robe
Black mortarboard hat
Sideburns and glasses
Textbook

Reception (as Professor)
White tux shirt
White bow tie
Black pants w/suspenders
White pique vest
Black tail coat
Black socks and shoes
Sideburns and glasses

Café (as Head Waiter)
Remove sideburns, vest & jacket
Black pants w/ suspenders
Black vest
Black bow tie
White waiter's apron
Moustache
Pewter arm bands

Avonlea Finale (as Mr. Sloane)
Green three-piece suit
Striped shirt w/ Eton collar
Green plaid tie
Watch and chain
Glasses
Scarf
Black bowler hat

ROYAL GARDNER / TOWNSPERSON
Avonlea (as Townsperson)
Light shirt – Eton collar

Brown vest & jacket
Brown pants
Black shoes and socks
Brown tie

Wedding
Same plus outerwear

ACT 2
Redmond, St. John Cemetery (as Roy)
Blue suit
Eton collar shirt
Vest

Reception (as Roy)
White wing collar shirt
Black tux pants / suspenders
White pique vest & bow tie
Black tail coat
Black shoes and socks
White gloves

Café (as Roy)
Blue suit
Charcoal coat
Scarf

Avonlea Finale (as Townsperson)
Same as Act 1

PAUL IRVING
Avonlea
Brown britches
Plaid shirt
Cap
Black boots and tights

Schoolhouse – Skating
Add grey heavy sweater and mitts

Wedding
Remove sweater
Light shirt/ Eton collar
Norfolk jacket
Long pants

ACT 2
Avonlea Finale
Same as Wedding – Act 1

FRED / ALONZO
Avonlea (Fred)
Beige linen shirt – Eton collar

Tweed jacket
Beige vest
Light brown pants
Bow tie

Wedding

Wing collar shirt
Grey/black striped pants
– with suspenders
Grey vest
Black cut-away frock coat
Black shoes
Black cravat
Top hat in hand

ACT 2

Redmond Campus (as Alonzo)

Brown pants
Beige linen shirt
Red sweater
Large bow tie

Reception (as Alonzo)

Wing collar shirt
White pique vest and tie
Black tux pants / suspenders
Black tailcoat
White gloves
Black shoes

Avonlea Finale (as Fred)

Same as Act 1
Add scarf

ANNETTA BELL / SOPHOMORE / DORM GIRL

Avonlea & Schoolhouse (as Annetta)

Black tights
Short cotton petticoat
Bloomers
Blue print dress with eyelet collar
Black boots

Wedding

Same with brown plaid shawl

ACT 2

Redmond Campus (as Sophomore)

Petticoat
Beige blouse
Beige skirt
Red cardigan sweater

Light tights and shoes
Pearl bracelet

Dressing Room (as Dorm Girl)
White tights
Crinoline
Pink ball gown
Light shoes
Hair ornament

GIRLS (CHORUS)

Avonlea (School Girl)
Bloomers
Short petticoat
Black tights and shoes
Beige pinafore
Beige print dress with lace trim

Wedding
Add shawl

ACT 2

Redmond Freshette (if needed)
Cream blouse
Long petticoat
Brown/beige checked skirt
Paisley vest
Shoes

Avonlea Finale
Same as Act 1,

BOYS (CHORUS)

Avonlea
Green plaid shirt
Taupe britches
Cap
Black tights
Black shoes

Wedding
Light shirt w/collar
Checked jacket,
Taupe britches
Scarf

ACT 2

Avonlea Finale
Same as Wedding, Act 1